Star Hatchling

Also by Margaret Bechard

My Sister, My Science Report
Tory and Me and the Spirit of True Love
Really No Big Deal

Star Hatchling

Margaret Bechard

Viking

For Lee

VIKING
Published by the Penguin Group
Penguin Books USA Inc., 375 Hudson Street, New York, New York 10014, U.S.A.
Penguin Books Ltd, 27 Wrights Lane, London W8 5TZ, England
Penguin Books Australia Ltd, Ringwood, Victoria, Australia
Penguin Books Canada Ltd, 10 Alcorn Avenue, Toronto, Ontario, Canada M4V 3B2
Penguin Books (N.Z.) Ltd, 182-190 Wairau Road, Auckland 10, New Zealand

Penguin Books Ltd, Registered Offices: Harmondsworth, Middlesex, England

First published in 1995 by Viking, a division of Penguin Books USA Inc.
Reprinted by arrangement with Penguin Books USA Inc.
10 9 8 7 6 5 4 3 2 1
Copyright © Margaret Bechard, 1995
All rights reserved

LIBRARY OF CONGRESS CATALOGING-IN-PUBLICATION DATA
Bechard, Margaret.
Star hatchling / Margaret Bechard   p.   cm.
Summary : The female-dominated culture of a distant planet
encounters human beings for the first time.
ISBN 0-670-86149-9 (hc)
[1. Science fiction.]   I. Title.
PZ7.B38066St 1995 Fic—dc20   95-18930 CIP AC

Printed in U.S.A.
Set in Korinna

Contents

1
To the River

I reached into the basket and pulled out a fat yala root. "Doesn't this one look just like Uncle Hasa?" I held it up for my cousins to see.

Shelum laughed. Shefa leaned over and drew a mouth in the yala with his claw tip. "Always talking."

I moved the yala from side to side and deepened my voice. "Keep your mind on your grippers and your grippers on your work."

Behind us, the door to the food house opened, and Uncle Hasa stepped out into the sunlight. Shefa and Shelum bent over their work, and I began scrubbing, hard, at the root's peel.

"Shem," Uncle Hasa said. He was holding a pair of water jugs.

I bent closer over the yala and closed my ear flaps. He might give the job to Shefa instead. Shefa might have to go to the river and fill the jugs.

"Shem!" Uncle Hasa clicked his claws.

I hissed, tossed the yala back into the basket and stood up. "Yes, Uncle Hasa."

"We need fresh water." He shook the jugs by their straps and I walked over and took them. My tail scratched across the sand, moving toward my feet. I stopped it before Shefa and Shelum could see.

"And don't waste time." Uncle Hasa pointed a claw at my cousins. "Always remember. Keep your mind on your grippers and your grippers on your work."

Shefa and Shelum blinked. "Yes, Uncle Hasa," they said.

As soon as he was back inside the food house with the door safely shut, they looked up at me, grinning. Shefa nudged Shelum. "Don't wander out of the Territory, Shem," he said.

"Don't let Outsiders get you," Shelum said, and they both fell about, laughing so hard they nearly knocked over the basket of yalas.

"Have fun scrubbing," I said, but that only made them laugh harder. I adjusted the jugs and started around to the front of the food house.

The sun was at its highest, and its light flooded the Clearing, its heat washing over my scales, warming my blood. It would be colder in the forest and by the river. I hated being cold. I hated going to the river alone. I hated being so close to the boundary of our Territory. So close to the claws of Outsiders.

Father and Uncle Sifesh were feeding the sheemos. They looked up as I passed the tanks.

"What are you supposed to be doing, Shem?" Father asked, his grippers resting on his claws.

"Fetching water."

"Hurry up, then. Idle feet mean empty bellies."

"And empty jugs mean dry pots," added Uncle Sifesh.

I hissed, but too softly for their flaps to catch. I started slowly across the Clearing, shuffling my feet in the sand.

The females were seated in a circle near the dining house. My mother, heavy with the eggs she would soon lay, sat at their center. Their voices quieted as I went by, and I knew they had been arguing again.

My younger sister, Cheko, left the circle and ran up beside me, her pet lasha clinging to her shoulder, its tail wrapped around her upper arm. "Going to the river, Shem?"

"Very good, Cheko. Where else would I be going with empty water jugs?"

Her tongue flicked out in a quick smile. "It wasn't the jugs that told me, Shem. It was your tail. But don't be scared. I'll come with you and protect you. Sitting in the sand talking about eggs is boring."

I glanced back at the other crestheads, but, of course, no one paid any attention. No one ever told Cheko what to do.

"I'm not scared," I said. And my tail slid away from my feet in a wide, comfortable arc. Cheko was bossy and Cheko was rude, but I did feel safer with her along.

"Carry this for me." She tossed a food pouch at me as she walked. I caught it and looked inside. It was full of dried tislit.

"What's this for?"

She tipped her head toward the lasha. "She gets hungry." The lasha looked at me with its bright, unblinking eyes.

I slung the food pouch over my free shoulder. Uncle Hasa would be furious if he knew Cheko was carrying around so many tislit for her pet. But I wasn't going to be the one to tell him.

I looked down at her, walking with her typical crest-head swagger, her claws slightly extended, her grippers folded across her chest above them, her tail curved high off the ground. The scales on her crest gleamed like polished stones. "Have you been waxing your crest?"

"What if I have?" She looked at me. "Why? Doesn't it look right?"

"Well . . ." I considered. "It's just such a small crest . . ."

She drew herself up to her full height, and she could nearly look me in the eye. "It is the exact size a crest should be on a female after her fourth molting. I asked Grandmother, and she said that it is so." Cheko clicked her claws, already bigger than mine, with larger hooks and points. "And I certainly am glad I don't have a great ugly flat head like a male."

The doors and windows of the sleeping house were closed and shuttered to hold in the heat. Uncle Simla was dozing in a patch of sunlight, his grippers still holding the elma skin he had been scraping. We circled to the back, toward the river path. Here, behind the houses, the shadows of the forest began to stretch long and dark across the ground. The upturned hatchling tanks, dry and cold, stood in the gloom near the compost.

Cheko stopped and I did, too. I thought of our mother and the eggs and the promise of new hatchlings. Hatchlings meant more work for me, but even I would be glad to see the tanks full, their waters churning with the shiny fins and the rounded backs. Uncle Simla had told us the stories of long ago. When all the crestheads laid eggs and almost all the hatchlings survived. When the sand of the Clearing had to be raked three and even four times a day, so many feet disturbed it. When the Family filled the basking rock, lying claw to claw and tail tip to tail tip in the bright sunlight. In my hatching, only the three of us, Shefa and Shelum and I, had lived to lose our fins and grow our legs. There had been more eggs and more hatchlings, but none had survived. And in Cheko's hatching, well, it had truly been Cheko's hatching alone. And no more had followed.

"They're arguing, you know," Cheko said, softly, "about whether or not I should come to the laying."

I flared my gills. "But you're too young. Two . . . no, three moltings too young."

"They know, but they're afraid." Cheko looked at the tanks and not at me. "They're afraid there won't be another laying for me to witness. There have been so few eggs."

I flicked my tongue, half-heartedly, and tried to sound encouraging. "You know how the Grown Ones are, Cheko. Always finding shadows in the forest. You don't have to worry."

She stiffened and moved away. "I'm not worried." She jerked at the straps on the jugs. "If we're going to the river, let's get going."

The mehtas grew thick beside the river path, and talfas leaned close, their leaves brushing the tops of our heads. It *was* colder in the forest, and even Cheko slowed down a little. We passed a shatalsha—its trunk so big that twenty grown males could not join grippers around it, its branches so high that they grew out of our sight. I opened my flaps, straining to hear its whispery voice. Only crestheads could hear the voice of the shatalsha, but I didn't think it hurt to try.

And not all the crestheads could hear the voice. I glanced at Cheko, wondering, but it didn't seem like a good time to ask.

Sooner than I was ready, the path began to run downhill, and we stepped from the protection of the trees onto the broad, open expanse of the riverbank. The rains had come on time this season, as if a branch of the Great Shatalsha had grown straight up to rip open the clouds and pour water upon us. Now the river swirled almost to the tops of its banks, and the skiffs bobbed and bumped against the dock. I didn't like looking across the water and seeing mehtas and talfas that were not in our Territory. I tried to uproot Uncle Simla's warnings of what would happen to anyone foolish enough to fall into the grippers of Outsiders.

Cheko sat down in a place where the sun, slanting through the trees, made a warm puddle. The lasha jumped from her shoulder and rolled and stretched. Cheko cleared the sand with her gripper. "Come play a game, Shem." She drew a line across the sand.

"I don't have time to play games, Cheko." But I moved closer. "Next line," I said.

She added another to her drawing and looked up at me. The lasha looked up at me, too.

I hissed. "Two more."

Her tongue flicked in a smile, and she drew two more lines.

"Next line," I said.

"That's five," she said, her flaps opening and closing as her digit drew the line. "Can't you guess it, Shem?"

"Is it . . . is it a skiff?"

She laughed, added her last line and said, "Wrong! It's a tislit! I win."

I dropped the food pouch and one of the jugs on the

sand. I uncorked the other jug. "I told you I don't have time to play silly games." I waded into the water, pushing through a patch of fragrant sheels growing near the shore. No one could beat Cheko at Next Line. Of course she was probably cheating. I held the jug under the water, bubbles rising and breaking against my legs. The river here was wide, wider even than the Clearing. If Outsiders attacked, they'd have to come in skiffs.

"Maybe I'll stay here," Cheko said. "When you go back."

She was lying flat now, all four arms and her legs and tail stretched out around her. Her membranes were up, protecting her eyes from the glare.

"You know you can't stay here alone," I said. I corked the jug and waded up the bank for the other one.

She lowered a membrane and looked at me. "I can if I want to."

I set the full jug on the sand and picked up the empty one. "You know what Mother would say," I said. "And Grandmother."

"Then you can just stay here with me." She looked across the river. "We can watch for Outsiders together. Outsiders with their long digits. And their big sharp claws." She tried to make her voice low and gravelly like Uncle Simla's.

I closed my flaps and waded back into the river. "I've seen the messenger who comes to call Grandmother to

Council, Cheko," I said, filling the second jug. Her claws hadn't been that big. Of course one Outsider wasn't like a whole family of Outsiders.

"Grippers to hold and claws to tear," Cheko said. And then she screamed, "Shem!"

"Oh, very funny, Cheko . . ."

"Look!" She was scrambling to her feet, spraying out sand, her grippers and claws pointing across the river. "Look!"

I spun around. "Is it Outsiders? Are they coming?" I rushed back to the shore, water splashing over my head as I ran.

Cheko grabbed my right claw arm and pointed up at the sky with her other gripper. "Do you see it?"

I saw a bright point of light, flying high above the far shatalshas. "Is it a mechaka?" I whispered.

Cheko laughed loudly, but her gills flared with excitement. "Don't be stupid, Shem. It's too big. And too shiny."

"Run, Cheko!" I pulled toward the trees, toward the Clearing. "Run!"

But she pulled me back, toward the light. "I think it's a star, Shem. A falling star."

It was coming closer. Getting bigger. And then my flaps were filled with a roaring, like nothing I had heard before, not from the wind in the shatalsha nor from the river at its strongest. I jerked my arm loose, and I threw myself facedown on the sand, with my flaps pressed tight against my head and both my lids and my membranes closed over my eyes.

The roaring passed over us. I heard Cheko cry out. I felt heat across my back. I smelled burning.

There was a great *thump* somewhere deep in the forest. The ground under me shook. And then all was still.

2
Not a Drill

I dug through the food tubes in the hopper, looking for one I hadn't tried yet. Shrimp and rice. No way. Beef stroganoff. Yuck. Who did they think was eating this stuff? I finally found one that said STRAWBERRY ICE CREAM. I slit it open and tried some. It wasn't totally awful, so I finished it and had another one.

I dropped the empty tubes into the cycler. A couple of dozen were already in there. If I'd been eating three meals a day, and I'd eaten four or five tubes, figuring food and water . . . I gave the cycler a kick. This reminded me of one of Dr. Cynthia Wu's favorite math problems. And, anyway, I'd been eating whenever I felt like it. There was no way I could figure out how long I'd been in this stupid escape pod by counting nourishment tubes.

"Forever, Hanna," I said out loud. "You've been in here all alone forever."

I walked back past the empty seats to the front of the

pod. Twelve paces exactly. I didn't even bother to count them this time. The viewport was still blank. I tapped a couple of the keys on the com, but nothing changed. The com wouldn't work. The radio wouldn't work. Even the stupid cycler wouldn't work.

When we'd been onloaded onto the *Alan Turing II,* Mom and Dad and Jeffrey and me and all the other colonists, Dr. Geraldo Wu had given us a tour of the whole spaceship. Our quarters and our stasis chambers. The crew decks and the Brussard catchers. And the escape pods. "Of course we don't expect to need these," Dr. Geraldo Wu had said. "The escape pods will only be used in the case of absolute emergency. And each pod will be staffed by trained personnel." I hadn't actually been paying a whole lot of attention that day, but I could access that part really well. Trained personnel. I turned around and looked at the seats and the equipment lockers and the food hopper. Just where were the trained personnel?

I slumped down into the nearest seat. "This is all your fault, Andrea Hadaka," I said. "All your stupid fault."

We had just finished a mandatory exercise period. All the kids in my stasis group, the most boring stasis group on the entire ship. I'd begged Mom to get us into the same group as the Montoyas, so I'd at least be awake with Melissa, but no. I was stuck with my little brother, Jeffrey, and Andrea Hadaka. Dr. Cynthia Wu had made us climb the ropes, and I was the only one who hadn't managed to make it to the top. Andrea had made her usual smart remarks, and I'd called her a slime mold, and Dr. Wu had given me a fifteen-minute lecture on cultural diversity, and then she'd announced that we all had to take one more look at the comdisc on positive attitudes toward indigenous life-forms.

There I'd been, trapped in this classroom with ten kids who all hated me. Except, as soon as Dr. Wu was gone, Jeffrey had said, "Let's play hide-and-seek." I would have groaned like everybody else—Jeffrey always wants to play hide-and-seek—but Andrea said, "Oh, no, Jeffrey. We have a responsibility to watch this comdisc." So right away I had to say, "Great idea, Jeffrey. You're It."

The escape pod had seemed like the perfect place to hide. I knew nobody else would think of it, because we weren't supposed to go into the pods except during the drills. It had been dark inside and quiet. It had been nice. You're never alone on a colony ship. Somebody is always around. Even when you come out of the bathroom, somebody's right there, waiting for their turn. It was nice to be all alone in the quiet and the dark. I'd been thinking about Ravenna Prime, and what all my friends back there were doing. And I'd been thinking about how much I knew I was going to hate the new planet when we finally got there. When the inner airlock had closed and the emergency lights had gone on, I'd nearly jumped right out of my skin. I'd never even heard the escape drill siren.

Only this wasn't a drill. This was the real thing. I knew that now. I leaned forward in the seat and pressed my face against the viewport, cupping my hands to block out the interior light. All I could see was my own reflection. But the other escape pods had to be out there. I knew they were out there. A Class-A colony ship had room in the pods for everybody, all the colonists and all the crew. "More than enough room," Dr. Geraldo Wu had said. Mom and Dad and Jeffrey were out there in one of the other pods. Jeffrey was probably whining and complaining about the food. They were probably trapped with Andrea Hadaka. I could feel tears itching at the corners of my eyes. I'd be glad to see even Andrea right now.

Although, when I thought about it, maybe it wasn't all her fault. When I thought about it, it was really Mom and Dad's fault. I'd told them we shouldn't leave Ravenna Prime. I'd told them space travel was dangerous. But no one would ever listen to me. "Think of it, Hanna," Mom had said. "The first Terran colonists of a new planet." And Dad had patted me on the head, which I hate, and he'd said, "It will be fun, Hanna. Better than any reality disc. It will be a *real* adventure."

"This is some fun, Dad," I said, and my breath smudged the plastic.

My stomach lurched and churned and my fingers squeaked upward across the viewport. I was floating in midair. Zero-grav! It was zero-grav! My first thought was, Oh, great. The artificial gravity is broken, too. But then I actually accessed some of the Basic Physics of Space Travel, something I'd thought I'd *never* need. Zero-grav

meant the engines had shut down. And the engines shutting down meant we were in orbit. Orbiting a planet.

I pressed my face back to the viewport, even though
I knew I wouldn't be able to see anything. Dr. Geraldo Wu
had said the com would search for the nearest blue-water
planet that could sustain Terran life. But I'd thought the
com was broken.

"Initiating planet-fall." The com's voice, booming out
all of a sudden, startled me. My hands slapped against
the viewport, and I shot off into the middle of the room.

"All personnel, commence proper procedures immediately."

All personnel. That was me. I swam my way over to
the nearest seat and gave myself a shove. Only I pushed
off way too hard and crashed into the back wall. I hated
free fall. I had to use the handholds to pull myself over to
the storage locker.

It was full of suits and boots. The first couple of suits
were way too big, but the third was smaller. I accessed
everything they'd told us in the last drill. How to keep
your arms and legs from tangling in the zero-grav. How to
seal the joints. How to get the helmet on before you slid
your hands into the thick gloves. The suit sort of bagged
above the boots, and my head banged around in the helmet. But I reminded myself that it was really just a precaution. Geraldo Wu had said the suits were really just a
precaution.

"Assume proper reentry positions."

"I am assuming as fast as I can!" I shouted. I swam back to the front, using the seats to haul myself along. I pulled myself down into a seat up front, my boots clanking hard against a control panel, and the harness snapped into place over my shoulders.

Pressure pushed me back, and it was hard to breathe, hard to push my lungs out against the heavy, invisible wall that was leaning against me. I closed my eyes and thought about what to say when I saw them all again. I'd be really calm. Really smooth. "Where have you guys been?" Or "What took you so long?" Or "That was an adventure?"

The pressure released, and my lungs sucked in a big breath of air. There was a shudder, a grinding of metal I could hear clearly. My head bounced around in the too-big helmet, and my nose crunched against the front.

My eyes watered with the pain. It took me a few seconds to realize that the harness had released. That we had landed.

"Initiate vehicle exit procedures."

I stood up, and the sudden weight nearly made me sit back down. Planetary gravity, I thought. And then, Get out! Get out!

I stumbled to the door and hit the release button. The door shushed open, and my ultraviolet visor slid down. I could see a big, flat cleared area, surrounded by things that might be trees. Really big trees. I couldn't see any of the other pods, but they must be on the other side, or even around front. Stay calm. That was the first rule Dr. Cynthia Wu had taught us.

I lowered myself slowly through the door. And for the first time in months, I was standing on solid ground.

I took a couple of steps and nearly tripped over my own feet. I wasn't used to being planet-side. Stay calm. I worked my way around the pod, running one glove along its surface. They did look like trees, those big things. I'd heard about trees. It was interesting to actually see them.

The other pods weren't on the other side. Only more trees. Nothing but trees. I shoved at the visor, but my gloves slipped on the smooth surface. "Mom!" I shouted. "Dad!" My voice echoed in the helmet. Calm, staying calm.

I turned, my feet heavy and slow in the clunky boots. They had to be here somewhere. The coms would have been programmed to find the same planet. Wouldn't they? Wouldn't they all be programmed to the same co-ordinates?

Don't panic, I thought. And as soon as I thought it, panic shot red hot into my brain.

I spun away from the pod, and I started to run. My hands out in front of me. My feet stumbling. Tears running down my face and neck, into the helmet's sealring.

"Mom!" I shouted again. I tripped. Felt my body flying. Felt it hit something, hard. My head thudded against the back of the helmet. For the first time since I'd left the *Alan Turing II,* I saw stars. Then I passed out.

3
Star Hatchling

Cheko grabbed me and hauled me to my feet. "Don't just lie there, sheemo brain. I want to find the star!"

I managed to grab the water jugs and the food pouch before she dragged me back into the forest. At the fork, she pulled me along the path that led away from the Clearing, the branch that led deeper into the forest. I opened my flaps to their widest, hoping to hear shouts or running footsteps. Someone else must have seen this thing falling from the sky. Someone else must have heard the thump and felt the ground shake. But the forest was silent. Not even the elmas were calling.

I dug my feet in and pulled Cheko to a stop. "Shouldn't we tell somebody? Shouldn't we tell Grandmother?"

Cheko fisted her grippers and rested them on her claws. "Shem. The most exciting thing that ever happened in this Territory was two seasons ago when Uncle Hamsha caught that huge tislit. A star is something different. A star is something worth seeing. If we tell, they'll just make us stay in the Clearing where it's safe."

I *wanted* to stay in the Clearing where it was safe. And what did she mean by "safe"?

The lasha rustled through the mehtas and leapt from the edge of the path to Cheko's shoulder. Cheko smiled. "See. Even lashas aren't scared."

At the next fork, we took the picking path. It was narrower and not so well traveled. We passed Uncle Hasa's shatalsha, and Uncle Hamsha's and Father's. Thoughts of Outsiders and their claws grew up the sides of my mind, like lisla creepers on the sleeping-house wall. "I think we should go back," I said.

"Not when we've come this far." Cheko stepped off the path and began to push her way through the mehtas.

"Cheko!" I hurried after her. Branches scratched my legs and roots caught at my feet. "Cheko, we can't leave the path!"

She paused and glanced back. "Why can't we leave the path, Shem?"

"Because . . . because we're not supposed to."

"All the more reason to do it," she said, her tongue flicking in and out. And she pushed farther into the underbrush.

I caught a branch just before it slapped me in the face. "I don't believe you even know where this star is."

"I wouldn't lead us off on a wild sheemo chase, Shem."

"Oh, yes you would, Cheko." I clicked a claw at her back, but quietly. "You just never think. That's your problem. Anything you want to say, you just go ahead and say it. Anything you want to do, you just go ahead and do it." The strap to the food pouch caught on a branch, and I had to stop to untangle it. "And who gets the blame? Me. I get the blame. And you—"

She stopped so suddenly I ran smack into her back and nearly stepped on her tail. She was moving her head from side to side, her eyes enlarged, her nostrils opening and shutting.

"See," I said, "you *have* gone and gotten us lost."

She hit me, hard, with the flat of her claw. "Be still! Use your nose, instead of your mouth!"

I smelled it at once. "Smoke!" I shrieked, and Cheko clamped her flaps shut.

"It's the star, Shem." One by one, Cheko pried my digits from her arm. "It's just the star." And she began to move deeper into the smell.

The smoke got thicker, seeping under our closed nostrils, making us cough. We passed patches of blackness, where small flames had tried to become fires. Leaves and creepers smoldered near our feet. "A good thing the forest is so wet," Cheko said.

And then, as the smoke became even thicker, eddying and swirling around us in currents of its own, we came upon a clearing. A clearing newly made in the heart of our forest. Some of the talfas were knocked over, the mehtas crushed and flattened. And a furrow had been cut, as if someone had taken the seed end of a giant rake and dug a huge planting row in the wet soil.

The lasha beeped once and was silent.

"That's a star?" I whispered.

At the end of the furrow lay a big, black lump. Dirt had sprayed up along its sides and across its back. Heat radiated from it, but no light. Only darkness.

"It's bigger than a sheemo tank," Cheko whispered.

"It's uglier than a sheemo tank," I whispered back.

We stepped a little farther into the clearing. A hole gaped in the star's near side. We could see more darkness inside.

"Stars are smaller than that, Cheko. Much smaller. And brighter. How can a star be so dark and ugly?"

Cheko hissed.

"And it smells," I said. "It smells of smoke and . . . and something bad. Something really bad." I tugged at her claw arm. "Let's go. Let's go back to our Clearing."

She stood up. I was afraid she was going to say no, that she would want to stay, would want to get closer. But she said, "All right. I guess it's *not* any more exciting than a big tislit."

I had turned, was already moving back the way we had come, when I saw it. And, before I could stop myself, I pointed and I said, "What is that?"

Cheko stopped, too. And she looked. And, of course, she went closer.

I edged up beside her and peered over her shoulder.

Something lay under a mehta, near the edge of the new clearing. Something bloated and white against the bright leaves and the soft dirt. "Is it some kind of plant?" I whispered. "It looks like a fungus. Or maybe tesla moss?" The biggest patch of tesla moss I'd ever seen.

Cheko didn't answer. She bent down, picked up a stick and poked the thing. I stepped back, ready to run.

The stick sank into the surface, making a small dent. But when Cheko pulled the stick back, the dent filled and disappeared. The thing didn't move or make a sound.

"I think it's some kind of animal," Cheko whispered.

"I think it's dead," I whispered back.

She looked at me, and her eyes glinted in a ray of the sun. "I think it came out of the star, Shem!"

I straightened and looked back at the smoking black hulk. I looked at the thing under the mehta. "*This* is what hatches out of stars?"

Cheko was kneeling down, pushing the branches aside. "Look. There are arms and legs. Don't you think so, Shem? Don't you think those are arms and legs?" The lasha jumped from her shoulder and sniffed at a foot.

I bent down to see better. "No claws. No tail."

Cheko was crawling farther under the mehta. "I bet there's a head," she said, her voice muffled by the leaves. "Go around and look, Shem."

"What?"

"The branches are in my way. Go on the other side and see if there's a head."

"I don't want to know if there's a head."

Cheko's face appeared between two branches. She clicked her claw. "Stop arguing."

I walked, slowly, to the other side of the mehta. I knelt down and shoved the lowest branches aside. There was something sort of like a head. It was round. It looked hard and heavy.

"Well?" Cheko was standing again, straining to see.

"There's something," I said. "It looks more like a rock than a head."

"A rock?"

I prodded it with my foot, and, surprisingly, the hatchling's whole body flipped over. I was staring down at my own face, swimming across the rounded surface.

I screamed and leapt back. My foot caught on a root, and I sat down heavily on my tail.

Cheko came running around the mehta. "What in the name of the Fruit . . ." She was silent. I moved beside her. Both our faces looked back up at us, the eyes big, the gills flared.

"A reflection," she said. "Like on water." But when she touched it with the tip of her claw, the claw clicked against an invisible barrier and did not slide beneath the surface.

We both took a step back.

"How does it do that?" I said, finally.

Cheko's gills flared even more. "It's wonderful, Shem. Isn't it wonderful?"

I closed my flaps. "I think it's awful."

Cheko laughed, and the noise sounded loud in the empty clearing. "Shem. You're afraid of your own tail."

I nudged the puffy shoulder with my toe. "This could be anything, Cheko. You don't know it fell from the Great Shatalsha. You don't know it hatched from the star." Fear washed over me, like a river overflowing its banks. "Maybe it's some new kind of Outsider."

Cheko laughed again, much louder. "Outsiders may be strange, Shem, but they're not this strange."

"We should throw it into the river," I said. "We should let the tislit have it." I rested my foot on the shiny round head to show Cheko that I was not afraid.

Under my foot, the head shifted and rolled from side to side. A low, rasping sound came from somewhere deep inside.

I couldn't move. Thorns of fear gripped tight and held me in my place.

Cheko shoved me aside. "Keep your big feet off it."

I was glad to move away, would have moved much farther, if I had dared. Cheko knelt in the dirt, bending over the thing like a father over a Tailless One. The star hatchling rolled to one side. It pushed with its grippers as if it were trying to get up, and it made a strange, muffled croaking.

"Cheko," I whispered.

The hatchling slumped back down and was still.

Cheko looked up at me. "We have to take it to the molting cave, Shem."

"The molting cave? Do you think it's ready to molt?"

She rocked back on her heels and her tail. "I want to hide it, sheemo brain."

"Hide it? Cheko. It's ugly. It smells. It's . . . it's not normal."

"I know. That's the best part." She stood and came closer to me. I could see myself, stretched and widened, in her eyes. "Promise me, Shem. Promise me you won't tell anyone about this."

"But . . ." I wanted to tell somebody. I wanted someone else to deal with Cheko and her star and its hatchling.

She put her gripper, lightly, on my arm. "I want it to be a secret, Shem. A secret between you and me."

Not an order barked from cresthead to flathead. Not a favor, granted grudgingly from sister to brother. A secret, held between us as equals.

"All right," I said. "I promise."

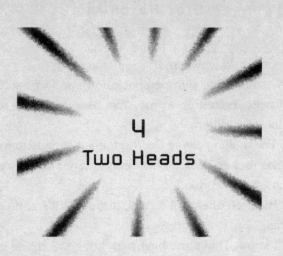

4
Two Heads

"You'll have to carry it," Cheko said.

I took a step backward and extended my claws. "Carry it?"

"It can't walk by itself, Shem." She clucked, and the lasha came to her. She picked it up and draped it on her shoulder.

"Well, I can't carry the star hatchling and the water jugs and the food pouch," I said.

Cheko looked at me, and for a moment, I thought I'd beaten her. Then she blinked. "All right. I'll carry the jugs and the pouch." She took them and arranged them awkwardly on her shoulders, the lasha digging its tiny talons into the straps. Seeing Cheko burdened like a flathead almost made up for having to carry the hatchling. Almost.

I bent down and grabbed it with both my grippers. My digits sank into the puffy, fibrous skin. The smell, like the smell of mehta berries left too long to ferment, filled my nostrils and my head. Trying not to think about what I was doing, I picked up the hatchling. It was about Cheko's height, only much fatter. I started to sling it onto my shoulder, but it was so light for its size, I misjudged and nearly tossed it right over my back. I had to grab it before it fell on its head.

"Be careful," Cheko said. "You don't want to hurt it." She started through the mehtas.

I hissed, but I didn't say anything. I finally managed to wiggle the star hatchling onto my shoulder. It was awkward to balance, and the round, hard head banged painfully against my back. Branches slapped us and mehta thorns caught at the puffy skin, but, seeing that Cheko was no longer watching, I did little to protect it.

When we reached the path, Cheko quickened her pace, and I had to run a little to keep up, in spite of my cold-slowed muscles. The head beat a constant rhythm against me.

"Slow down," I panted.

"We don't want anyone to see us," she said, and I was glad to hear that she was panting, too.

The picking path soon branched into the path to the molting cave. We were many shatalsha lengths from the Clearing, well hidden from inquisitive eyes and flaps. The path was overgrown, and we had to push through low-hanging branches. Then the talfas thinned, and, abruptly, we came to the Clearing in front of the molting cave.

No one had been here in some time. The next molting would be for Shefa and Shelum and me, and I could tell by my scales that the time would not come for several seasons. Small mehtas and talfa saplings sprouted around the Clearing. An older talfa had recently fallen, and its trunk ran the length of the Clearing.

It made me sad, a little, to see the Clearing so overgrown and untended. "Someone should see to this," I said, knowing I sounded like Uncle Hasa, and knowing that there were no grippers to spare for such a chore.

"It's exactly what we need," Cheko said. The lasha leapt from her shoulder to the trunk of the talfa. Cheko plunked down the jugs and the pouch.

I let the star hatchling slide to the ground. It sprawled limply at my feet. It looked dead. Of course, mechakas looked dead, too, just before they jumped up and bit you.

Cheko had disappeared into the cave. She poked her head back out. "Bring it here, Shem."

I was too tired to pick it up again. I didn't even want to touch it, to feel its rough, raspy skin against my scales.

"Hurry up, Shem!"

I flexed my digits and wrapped them around both sides of the head. It was cold and smooth, smoother even than a rock taken from the river. But touching it didn't make my tail twitch like touching the skin did. I tightened my grip and pulled. The hatchling slid along the ground.

I backed toward the cave, hunched over, dragging my burden after me. This was much easier. And it smelled better. I pulled harder. The hatchling stopped sliding.

I jerked at it, but it was stuck fast. A flap of the skin was caught on a rock or a mehta sprout. I said a word Father said when the tislit boiled over. Then I pulled again, leaning back, my digits twisting with the effort. The head turned against them. There was an odd, grating noise and a soft sigh.

The resistance was gone. I stumbled backward, my claws snapping with surprise. My digits flexed convulsively, and I nearly dropped the head.

The head!

My grippers held the smooth, hard head. But the body was still lying on the ground.

I flung the head away from me and closed my eyes and my flaps.

Behind me, I heard Cheko shout. "Hey! Watch what you're . . . Was that the head? Did you just throw the head at me?"

Her digits dug into my claw arm, as painful as sheemo teeth. I opened my eyes and turned to face her. "I'm sorry, Cheko. I didn't mean to. Really. It was an accident."

But she wasn't paying any attention to me. Her eyes were focused behind me, her flaps opened to their widest, and her gills were flared.

I opened my own flaps. Something was scratching

on the ground. Something was coming closer and closer to us. The lasha scuttled across my feet to crouch under a mehta.

I turned around, slowly.

The headless hatchling was crawling across the ground.

I screamed, and Cheko screamed, and, clutching each other, we stumbled into the cave.

Cheko pulled me to a halt before we crashed into the back wall. "Wait," she gasped. "Wait."

Outside, in the Clearing, I could hear something rattling and scraping. Cheko took a shuffling step toward the light. "Cheko. No. Don't."

"I have to look, Shem."

Hanging onto her arm, I moved with her to the cave's mouth. Together we peered out into the brightness.

"It *has* a head," Cheko whispered.

The hatchling was up on its knees and its grippers. Or what had to be its knees and its grippers. And Cheko was right. It did have a head. Smaller than the first and rougher. But definitely a head.

My gills flared. A tail tip, of course, would be nothing. Anybody could regenerate a tail tip. And Father, once, had regenerated a whole digit, bitten off by an enraged sheemo. But a head.

To grow a whole new head. And so fast!

The hatchling moved forward on its knees, and

Cheko and I, still clutching each other, stepped back. The hatchling's grippers swept the ground in front of it. Its little head moved from side to side. It looked, for all the Great Shatalsha, as if it were searching for something. Or someone. Maybe searching for someone who'd pulled off its first head.

Then it pushed against the ground and stood upright. Its head looked ridiculously small on top of the puffy body. I could see its tiny eyes and tiny mouth. Its grippers, fat and pale, clasped around its sprout-thin neck. Its mouth—hardly as big as one of my nostrils—opened. The tiny eyes grew a little bigger.

And when it seemed that the whole forest waited with ear flaps open, finally the mouth made a noise. An amazingly loud and piercing noise for such a little mouth. A noise that hurt my flaps and awoke the mechakas in the branches above us. Then the hatchling dove toward its old head, still spinning where I had thrown it.

Cheko and I had to lean out of the cave to watch. The hatchling picked up its old head, peered inside and shook it. Then it tried to fit the old head over its new head. But something was wrong, because it jerked the old head off. Then it sat down on the ground, cradling the old head in its lap, and the mouth made an eerie, keening noise. My tail twitched in the dark and bumped against Cheko's.

"I don't suppose," I said, "we could go get Grandmother now?"

Her eyes were shining and her gills were flared. Her tongue flicked out. "Don't be silly, Shem. This is just getting good." And she started out of the cave.

I grabbed her. "Where are you going?"

"Out there, of course."

"Out there? You can't go out there!" The star hatchling had been frightening when I'd thought it was dead. Now it was absolutely terrifying.

"Shem." Cheko put a gripper on my arm. "I can't tame it if I'm in here, and it's out there."

"Tame it?" My voice echoed off the walls of the cave, and Cheko closed her flaps.

"You're hurting my flaps, Shem."

"You can't tame that!"

She blinked. "I tamed the lasha, didn't I? Even though everybody said I couldn't."

She was right. Everyone had been amazed when Cheko had taught the lasha to eat from her gripper. Uncle Simla had said that Cheko talks to the animals. "But lashas are different," I said. "Lashas don't hatch out of stars."

Her tongue rolled out in a big grin. "But that's good, Shem. Getting them young like this makes it much easier. You don't know . . ."

Her voice trailed away. The hatchling was standing at the mouth of the cave, its head bent down to its shoulder. It made a noise, like the harsh croaking of a mechaka.

Cheko stepped forward, and the hatchling stepped back. I followed them both out into the sunlight.

Cheko extended her flattened grippers. "Nice hatchling," she said, in the soft crooning voice the uncles use to calm the sheemos. "Nice star hatchling."

The hatchling watched her with its tiny eyes. They were brightly colored, with hardly any darkness at all, and as they followed Cheko's slow movements, they reminded me of tislit darting through sunlit water. Long, dark, mossy strands grew out of the top of its head, and even more strangely, little short tufts grew over the eyes.

"Such a nice hatchling," Cheko murmured again. She was quite close now, close enough to reach out and touch the moss.

The mouth opened, and it showed all of its flat teeth.

Cheko jumped back, and I put my gripper on her shoulder. "Maybe you shouldn't try to make pets out of animals that are so big, Cheko."

She looked at me. "Shem. This is going to be a long, patient process. If you're going to panic at the least little thing, you'd better go back to the Clearing now."

The hatchling sat down, suddenly, its back resting against the fallen talfa's trunk. It looked comically like Uncle Simla, leaning against the sleeping-house wall. Its gaze moved from Cheko to me and back to Cheko. Its teeth were still bared, but if it had had a tail to curl and flaps to close, I would have said it looked more scared than angry.

"I don't want to leave you here alone, Cheko," I said, finally.

She blinked, and I wondered if she was just a little relieved. "All right then," she said, "get me the food pouch and try to stay out of the way."

5
Molting

Cheko sat down across from the hatchling, not too far away, but not too close, either, I noticed. I brought her the food pouch and the water jugs.

The lasha slipped out from under the trunk of the talfa. It sidled close to the hatchling and delicately sniffed one of the thick, fat feet. The hatchling looked at the lasha. I thought it was going to make that piercing noise again, and I closed my flaps. But it just pulled its feet closer to its body. The lasha stretched out next to Cheko's leg.

"This may take a while, because he is a flathead." Cheko pulled a large tislit from the pouch. "But the first thing you have to do is make the animal trust you." She held out the tislit. "So you feed it."

She waved the tislit enticingly at the hatchling. "Good star hatchling." The hatchling's head followed the motion of the tislit, back and forth, back and forth. "Nice star hatchling. Pretty star hatchling." His head continued to move, but he didn't try to take the tislit.

Cheko hissed. "Just how stupid can he be?"

With a loud beep, the lasha pounced. Its tiny teeth sank deep into the tislit and dragged it right out of Cheko's digits.

All three of us—Cheko, the hatchling, and I—jumped to our feet. The lasha crouched in our midst, hunched over its prize, growling deep in its throat. And the hatchling made an answering noise, deep in his throat.

"Stop it!" Cheko clicked her claw at the lasha, and the hatchling stepped back. He made a small squeaking sound. Cheko snatched the tislit out of the lasha's jaws and shoved the little animal aside with her foot. "Shoo! Scat!" The lasha slunk a short distance away.

The hatchling lifted a gripper. Cheko and I stood very still. But the gripper just wiped above the hatchling's eyes, and I saw that big drops of water were dripping from the edges of the long moss on the top of his head, dripping down the sides of his face. It made me thirsty, and I remembered the water.

I picked up the jug, pulled the stopper, and took a drink. I set the jug down carefully, but it tipped in the soft dirt, and precious water ran out.

"You sheemo brain!" Cheko and I both reached for the jug.

But the hatchling got it first. He scooped it up and

scuttled back against the trunk. He held the jug close and made the growling noise in his chest again.

Neither of us moved.

The hatchling shook the jug. He peered inside. He poured a thin trickle out onto his gripper.

"Hey!" Cheko said.

The hatchling raised his gripper to his mouth, and a short, fat tongue slid out and licked at the water. He looked directly at Cheko and me. He made his croaking noises. His shoulders moved up and down, as if he were adjusting his scales. Then he tipped his head back and drank. His eyes closed, and he made a noise that sounded so close to real speech, it made my tail curl. The hatchling looked right at me and displayed all his teeth in an angry grimace.

"Watch out, Shem," Cheko whispered. "I don't think he likes you."

He set the water jug down. He made another series of croaks. And then, right there in front of us, he began to molt.

Cheko hissed and grabbed my claw arm, and I blinked. Molting. The hatchling was definitely molting. Of course, not everybody just peels the skin right off their grippers. Not everybody just opens up the front of their skin and steps right out of it.

In less time and with less effort than it would have taken me to clean a tislit, the hatchling was out of his old skin.

"Like us," Cheko whispered.

I remembered my own moltings. How good it had felt to finally be free of the tight, cracking old skin. How my new skin had seemed to swell and fill with my enlarged body. I shut and opened my ear flaps. "But he's smaller than he was before."

He was much smaller. Not shorter, but thinner. Much thinner. And prettier. The new skin was not pale and puffy. It was smooth and shiny, the color of ripe shatalsha fruit. The face had remained the same, the color of an elma's underbelly, with those tislit eyes, still staring at us.

"Of course he was molting," Cheko said. "What else could it be?" She touched the discarded skin with her toe.

I almost said that it reminded me of the mechaka skin cloak Grandmother wore when she went to meetings of the Council. But I bit back the words. Cheko would only tell me to stop being ridiculous.

The hatchling wiped his gripper across his forehead again. And then he sat back down in the dirt, resting against the trunk.

"Good, good!" Cheko said. She sat back down, too, and held the tislit out.

I hissed. This *was* going to take patience. And what if Cheko could talk to only some of the animals? What if she didn't talk to animals that hatched from stars? The smell of tislit was making me hungry. I took a small one out of the pouch and popped it into my mouth.

The hatchling made a small choking noise. A digit extended toward the tislit in Cheko's gripper. Then more of the small, fat digits came out and, carefully, delicately, took the tislit.

I hunkered down beside Cheko. "Did you see how those digits bend?" I whispered.

"Hush," Cheko said. "Hush."

She was holding herself perfectly still, watching the hatchling. He didn't snarl and gobble at the tislit, as the lasha had. He bit off one, tiny corner. He showed all his teeth in that fierce grimace, and made more noises.

"I don't think he likes dried tislit," I said.

"But he ate." Cheko rolled out her tongue in a grin. "He ate from my gripper."

As Cheko's tongue came out, the hatchling stopped making his noises. The rest of the tislit hanging from his gripper dropped to the ground.

"He didn't eat much," I said.

"It's a start. A good start. You can't rush these things."

The hatchling was still staring at her, his eyes big and his mouth open. Cheko smiled again, and the hatchling squeaked. "That's enough for one day," Cheko said. "We should let him rest." She crossed the clearing to a talfa that grew among the mehtas and clipped a long lisla creeper with her claw. She tied one end to a branch of the fallen talfa. The other end she tied to the hatchling's leg, just above his foot. He made no attempt to stop her. Nor did he try to avoid her gripper as it patted him on the moss on his head.

"That lisla isn't going to hold him, you know." I tossed the tislit he had dropped to the lasha. "Those digits can untie that knot."

She laughed. "He's a flathead, Shem." She looked around the clearing. "We'll have to come back first thing tomorrow. To bring him more tislit and water."

I hissed. "I can't come back tomorrow. I have work to do. We can leave him a water jug."

Cheko had her grippers on her claws again. "I thought Uncle Hasa needed that water. For sheels or chlafa nodes or . . ."

"Yalas!" I shouted. I grabbed both the water jugs. No time to go all the way back to the river. How was I ever going to explain this?

Cheko caught up with me on the picking path. "Slow down," she said. The lasha was bouncing on her shoulder, its tail swinging wildly. "I was just thinking, Shem. Can you imagine all their faces when I bring the hatchling to the Clearing? I mean, when he's completely tame?"

My tail twisted closer to my feet. I could imagine it. I could imagine it all too well.

The picking path brought us into the Clearing by the food house. I braced myself to face Uncle Hasa's anger, raking my mind for a good excuse.

It was Grandmother who walked across the sand toward us. Even worse.

She walked right past me. "We've been looking everywhere for you, Cheko. Your mother says it is time to go to the Nesting Place. You will come with us."

I flared my gills, but Cheko said, quietly and calmly, "Yes, Grandmother." She started after Grandmother, then turned and came back to me. "You have to bring him food and water tomorrow," she whispered. She put her gripper on my claw arm. "And don't forget your promise."

Uncle Hasa's anger was lost in the excitement of preparing pouches of tislit and jugs of fermented mehta berries for the crestheads to take with them. Without the crestheads there, the last meal that night was simple, just some cold boiled tislit and the yalas. There was no hurry to clear, and the uncles lingered on the benches. Uncle Hasa told the story of the tislit who loved a mechaka. And Uncle Sifesh told how the sheemos tricked the Outsiders. When the laughter had died away, Uncle Simla rose slowly from his place, and we all fell silent to hear his familiar words.

"The first seed fell, in the rich and fertile soil of the first Clearing. And from that seed, the Great Shatalsha sprouted. It thrived and grew tall, pushing upward, through the darkness and past the seasons. And when it stood, straight against the sky and strong enough to bear the weight, the Great Shatalsha called forth from the darkness the sun and the moons and all of the stars to make their never-ending journeys upon its branches." Uncle Simla paused and looked around the table. Beside me, Shefa and Shelum leaned forward, eager to catch the words in their flaps. "In the fullness of time, in the proper season, the Great Shatalsha brought forth the one perfect fruit to hang on its lowest branch, closest to its roots. The one perfect fruit that bears our forest and our Clearing and all of the Family."

A small sigh of satisfaction swirled around the table as the story ended. But I felt a small sharp thorn of fear. Where on the Great Shatalsha were creatures that hatched from stars?

Father reached out and rubbed my head. "Don't worry about your mother and the eggs, Shem-la," he whispered. "Everything will be all right."

6
Coming On-Line

It took me a couple of seconds to figure out what was going on. "Hey, you guys." I spat out the disgusting thing they'd fed me. "Wait!" But they just went tromping off into the bushes, and by the time I'd unfastened the vine from my ankle, they had disappeared completely.

"Stupid Indigies," I muttered. Leaving me here in the middle of nowhere. Where was the pod? And where was everybody else? "Mom!" I yelled. "Dad! Dr. Wu!"

I yelled until my throat hurt. Then I sat down in the dirt. "Stay calm, Hanna. You have to try and stay calm." I took a big, deep, sort-of-shaky breath, and for a second, the smells were overwhelming, the trees, and the dirt, and just everything around me. I'd been so used to the canned air on the *Turing,* I'd forgotten what planet-side air was like. It made my head swim, and I would have sat down if I hadn't already been sitting. I held my hands on each side of my head to keep it steady, and I tried to stay calm and think at the same time.

The first thing was, I had to get out of the UV rays. It was so hot, and the sun was so bright, small but really bright. I knew the radiation levels had to be bad. Plus, my shirt was soaked with sweat. I collected the suit and the helmet and carried everything into the cave. It was dark in there and cool, and I felt a little better right away. I sat down, not too far from the mouth, and I tried to access Dr. Cynthia Wu's other rules. Stay calm. Go slow. Analyze your situation.

I was calm. I was going so slow I wasn't going anywhere. Analyze? My head ached. Maybe from the air, but maybe from bumping it inside the helmet. Nothing else seemed to be hurt or broken. Drinking the Indigies' water had been dumb, but I'd been *so* thirsty. I should have waited until somebody could test it and make sure it was okay. "But who's going to test it, Hanna?" I asked out loud, and my voice echoed around the cave and made me jump. At least I hadn't actually eaten the food stick thing. I ran my tongue over my teeth and gums. I couldn't feel any swelling or stinging. Maybe I could risk swallowing the stuff next time. If there was a next time.

Had I made the Indigies mad somehow? I'd tried to do everything we'd learned on the Cultural Arts comdisc. I hadn't screamed when I'd first seen them. I'd participated in their food and drink rituals. I'd even let them tie me up. I thought I'd been doing really great, except maybe for when the one with the big claws stuck out his tongue. Dr. Geraldo Wu had said, "The probability of finding an indigenous sentient life-form is infinitesimal." Why couldn't I get cute fuzzy ones, like Darwix? I thought. Why did I have to get the ones with claws?

I pulled the suit closer and started going through the pockets. I knew I wouldn't find a comtrans. If they weren't expecting us to meet Indigies, then they wouldn't equip the suits with communication devices. I found the personal transponder though, in the right front pocket.

"Just a simple homing device," Dr. Cynthia Wu had said. "Anyone can operate it." I keyed the on switch. Nothing happened. No beeping. No visuals. I keyed the switch again. Off, on. Off, on. Still nothing. I tapped the screen with my finger. "Come on," I said. "You're supposed to locate the other transponders." Nothing.

I took it out of the cave, thinking maybe outside it would work better. Nothing. I shook it, then slapped it hard against my leg. Still nothing. I tried to access everything Dr. Cynthia Wu had told us, although the trouble was I hadn't really been paying a lot of attention. They'd told us so much, and most of it was so boring. There was something about range. I could access Dr. Cynthia Wu standing at the front of the gym, and I had been giggling about her hair, and wishing Melissa were there to giggle with me, and Dr. Wu said something about range. I shook the transponder again. "They're just out of range," I said. "But they're here somewhere."

I clipped the transponder to my belt, making sure it was in the receive mode. The other Terrans would be looking for me. Mom and Dad would make them look for me. I wiped sweat out of my eyes and headed back to the cave. The vine was still lying on the ground. I carried the end into the cave with me, and I tied it back around my ankle. Because the Indigies were all I had.

When they came back, I'd explain to them who I was. I'd get them to take me to the escape pod. They could probably get the radio working. Or maybe they even had radios of their own. I knew they were pretty primitive-looking, but you were never ever supposed to judge by appearances. I mean, slime mold looks, well, exactly like slimy mold. But they have space travel. These Indigies had to have at least *radios*.

I made myself as comfortable as I could on the suit, and I fell asleep right away.

When I woke up, the sun was already up again, and it was hot. I stayed in the cave as much as possible. I only went out when I absolutely had to. Mostly to check the transponder. There wasn't much else to do except sit there and think. I tried to imagine what Melissa would say when I told her I'd spent almost a whole day doing nothing but sitting and thinking. I tried to imagine what Mom and Dad would say. I spent a lot of time thinking about them. How glad they'd be to see me. And how sorry they'd be to have put me through all this. "It's all our fault, Hanna," they'd say. "You were right. We never should have left Ravenna Prime."

When I heard the rustling in the bushes, the first thing I thought was that it was them, it was Mom and Dad. But it wasn't. One of the Indigies came through the bushes. I was glad to see it was the one with the smaller claws.

I stood up and went out into the sunlight, shading my eyes against the incredibly hot glare. Access your comdiscs, Hanna, I thought. He's not ugly. Just different. "Hi," I said. I tried to smile and look welcoming. "Why don't you sit down?" I waved my hand toward the ground in the shade of the branches. I tried to access all their rituals, tried to access if there was something they'd done that I needed to do now.

Little Claws moved closer, his feet shuffling and his tail getting in his way. He almost reminded me of the frilled grebol Jeffrey had wanted to buy when we'd stopped on Singapore Second or maybe it was New Nairobi—I couldn't access. The grebol would creep up to you like that when it was begging for a treat. I'd thought the grebol was really cute. Of course, the grebol hadn't been taller than me.

Little Claws stopped about a meter in front of me. I could smell him now. He smelled, different, I told myself.

He was holding a bag in his . . . not his paws, I thought. His hands. They were sort of like hands. Hands with long, long fingers. He opened the bag and set some of the food stick things on the ground between us. A water container swung on his shoulder. "I'm really thirsty. Thirsty," I said, slowly and clearly, and I pointed at the container, and I ran my tongue over my lips, to try to show what I meant.

Little Claws jumped back as if I'd hit him. Big, feathery fans opened out from the sides of his neck.

"Water?" I said, pointing to the container and licking my lips again. And I couldn't help thinking, *Just how dumb is this Indigie anyway?*

Little Claws' mouth opened. And then his tongue started sliding out, long and dark and bumpy. It kept coming and coming, slithering toward me.

I couldn't help it. I screamed, and we both sort of fell backward, away from each other. "Don't . . . stop . . ." I took a deep breath, trying to access everything the Wus had told us, everything I'd learned on all those comdiscs. I forced my mouth back into a smile, a big, nonthreatening, happy smile.

Little Claws stepped closer and opened his mouth, too. The tongue stayed in, but I could see all kinds of teeth, all kinds of sharp, pointed teeth. Then his claws came up, level with his hands, and he snapped both of them open and shut, close to my face.

I screamed again. I moved back, getting ready to run, but Little Claws moved in, blocking my escape. "Don't," I whispered. My legs gave way, and I sat down on the ground.

Little Claws towered over me, his mouth open, his claws open.

I tried to think of anything anybody had ever said that covered this. "Stay calm," I said out loud. "Go slow. Slow."

The flaps beside his eyes opened.

"Easy," I whispered. "Nice and slow and easy."

The flaps stayed open, but the mouth closed and so did the claws. Very slowly, he sat down across from me.

"Good Indigie," I whispered. "Nice Little Claws." I could see myself reflected in his enormous black eyes. I concentrated on my reflection. "Pretty Indigie. Easy, slow." I tried to make it kind of like a little song. The food sticks were scattered on the ground between us. I reached out, hooked one with my fingers and pulled it closer to me. I knew Little Claws was watching me, but he didn't move. "Easy, steady, good Indigie." I held the food flat on the palm of my hand.

The three long, pale, snaky fingers came forward, gently swept the food from my palm, and put it into his mouth.

I took a breath. "Good Little Claws." I snagged another piece of food. "Easy, slow."

The fingers came out again, and then something shifted in those deep black eyes. We both froze, our hands outstretched. The fans flared out, and Little Claws jerked his hand back. He hissed.

I sat very, very still. But he didn't move toward me,

didn't open his claws or his mouth, and when I held the food out again, he took it. He didn't eat it, though. He just held it closed up inside his hand and stared at me.

Then he hissed again. And he bent and picked up the water jug and offered it to me.

I grabbed it and drank, filling my mouth so full and so fast that water sloshed down my chin and into my collar. I splashed some on my hands and rubbed them across my face, and it felt cool and clean and wet.

I offered Little Claws the jug, and he poured some in his mouth. I realized I was hungry, and I broke the last piece of food into two pieces and offered him the bigger one. He pointed to the smaller piece. "No, no, really. I'm not that hungry. You can have the big one."

And I realized we were networking! He was on-line! I put my hand flat on my chest. "My name," I said, "is Hanna. And I need to find . . . wait." I jumped up and snapped a twig off the fallen tree, and I hunched back down and started drawing. "This is the pod, see, that I came in. It looks just like this. Well, sort of like this. And I need to find it. I need you to work the radio." I said "radio" loudly and clearly, and I waved the twig a little bit because I was getting excited.

Little Claws looked at the drawing in the dirt, and he looked at me, and he looked at the twig, and I thought that maybe I'd gone a little too fast. I put my hand on my chest again, and I said, "Hanna?"

He blinked, slowly and stupidly, and I thought, Great. He's totally off-line.

But then he put his hand on his chest and he said something.

"Oh," I said. "Oh. Is that your name? I mean . . ." And I tried to say it, only I knew it didn't come out right, I knew I was spitting too much or something.

Slowly, he reached over and took my hand, still holding the twig, and held it against my chest. His hand felt big and warm and scratchy, but I didn't flinch or pull away. He made a sound.

"Hanna," I said, and I nodded and smiled. "Hanna."

7
The Star

"Twig? Your name is Twig?"

His head bobbed up and down, making his moss swing. His gripper felt soft and warm, squishy like an overripe shatalsha fruit. I dropped it and resisted the urge to wipe my own gripper.

He pointed down at the drawing in the dirt.

Stay calm, Shem, I told myself. Just stay calm. Everything was happening too fast. I'd been almost disappointed when I'd found the hatchling still in the cave. I'd been hoping that he had untied the knot. I'd been hoping that, even though he was a flathead, he'd figured out how to get away.

When he had tried to tame *me*, I'd started to get scared. This wasn't happening the way it was supposed to. I was just supposed to be feeding Cheko's pet while she was gone.

But when he'd started playing Next Line . . . when he'd started playing Next Line . . . My mind rocked and tipped like a skiff in rapids. I gave myself a shake, from tail tip to claw tip. "Think, Shem," I whispered.

He played the game all wrong, of course. They played it all wrong . . . wherever he'd learned to play it. He'd drawn all the lines at once, and he hadn't given me a chance to guess.

He was still pointing at the drawing, pointing and looking up at me as if I were supposed to guess now. But it was easy now. The whole thing was right there. "Your star," I said. "You drew your star."

His head bobbed and bobbed, and he said something else. I knew he was saying something. He stood up. His grippers reached out and closed around my gripper arm, and he pulled me to my feet. He said something again, and then pointed across the clearing toward the path.

Why wasn't Cheko here now, when everything was going wrong? I felt a flood of pure, hot anger. This was all Cheko's idea. This was all her fault.

Twig bent and untied the lisla creeper from his leg. And I wasn't the least bit surprised. He pointed back to his drawing. He pointed at the mehtas where I had walked through.

"You want to go to your star?"

I knew what I should do. I should grab him right now and drag him right straight back to the Clearing. I should give him over to Father and Uncle Hasa and let them worry about him. He would be their problem then. Cheko would have to explain it all to them.

Twig moved across the clearing. He stopped at the mehtas and looked back at me. He said something, and the skin above his eyes puckered and wrinkled and then, amazingly, smoothed flat again. He swung the moss up and away from his eyes. And then he made that sound, the sound that is almost "Shem."

"All right," I said. "I'll take you to your star." I knew Cheko would be furious that I'd let him go. But I didn't care.

When we reached the path, he stopped and looked up at me, his eyes bright. They blinked once, fast. He pulled something from the strap at his waist. I thought it was a rock, and then I thought he was going to hit me, and I stepped back. But he held the thing in his gripper, turning first one way, than another on the path. Then he extended the thing up toward me, holding it out, offering it. It was shaped like the box Father had carved to hold his favorite knife, only much smaller. Its surface was covered with strangely shaped bumps and flat places. It gave off a sharp, burned odor that made my nostrils close and reminded me of the star. Twig said something and tapped at the flat place with his digit. I closed my flaps. "No. I don't want it. You keep it."

Twig said something, and his shoulders moved up and then dropped down again. He pointed down the path and made the same sound he'd made when he pointed at the drawing. "This way," I said.

The star still crouched, black and ugly, at the center of its clearing. The fires were gone, but the smell of smoke was heavy in the air, smoke and the smell that hurt my nostrils and curled my tail.

Twig pushed in front of me. He ran to the opening in the side of the star and poked his head inside. Then, before I could speak, he had pulled his body up and in and disappeared into the star's belly.

I moved closer to a low-growing talfa. There was a crash inside the star, and Twig appeared in the opening. He looked around, his skin wrinkled again. His face smoothed when he saw me. He raised his gripper and gestured.

"Me?"

Twig spoke, his voice loud, sharp. And his gripper gestured again.

Fear rooted me close to the talfa, but something else prodded at me, pushed me forward. A small voice, as soft as I imagined the voice of the shatalsha, whispered at the back of my mind, "Just one look. It can't hurt to look." What a story to tell the Young Ones when I was as old as Uncle Simla.

What a story to tell Cheko.

The star loomed above me, almost as tall as the food-house roof. The smell was much stronger, close up. Perhaps this was why Twig had such small nostrils. I touched the side. It was smooth and hard, dry and surprisingly warm under my digits. I pulled my gripper back and peeked inside the opening.

It was almost as dark as it had been inside the cave. I opened my eyes wider and saw Twig standing at one end. He was leaning over a long, narrow table or bench, and he was pushing at the surface.

Light suddenly flooded out of a small opening in the ceiling. The glare was intense, nothing like the light from sheemo oil lamps. More like a tiny sun, captured and imprisoned in the hole above my head. I raised my membranes to protect my eyes and raised my gripper to feel the heat. But there was no heat.

Twig turned and said something, showing me his teeth. Then he pointed at the tabletop.

I lifted myself through the opening. The floor was cold and hard under my feet, with strange bumps and protrusions. I had to duck my head away from the low ceiling. Several benches took up most of the space. They had high backs, and I wondered where you'd put your tail, and then I hissed at my mistake. The benches were crossed by thick, flat straps, like the straps we wove from strips of elma skin to carry the pouches and jugs. Only these did not look like the skin of any animal I knew.

I moved closer to Twig, who seemed, all at once, comfortingly familiar. He pointed again at the tabletop and said something. Then he stepped back and gestured me forward, gestured me closer.

More holes were inset into the table. They were filled with tiny lines, tiny drawings I couldn't understand. I leaned forward and something clicked under my gripper. I jumped back, as if I had been burned, although everything here was so cold, so lifeless.

Twig pointed toward a darker area of the table. He said something, making one sound slowly and loudly. His eyes looked up into mine. He put his gripper on my gripper arm and made the sound again. He wanted something, expected something.

"It's very nice here," I said. I moved my gripper toward the table, the benches, the light in the ceiling. "But I really have to go now. Father thinks I'm scrubbing hatchling tanks."

Twig spoke, his mouth twisting, his words harsh and guttural. He tapped his digits, hard, on the tabletop and looked at me. He pointed from me to the table and back to me.

Very carefully, I reached out and tapped a digit on the cold, slippery surface. "It's a nice table," I said. "It must be easy to keep clean."

Twig made a loud noise. Then he banged both his grippers down on the table. I thought I heard something crack, although the dark surface did not change. He looked at me, waiting, expecting again.

I banged my grippers down, too, as hard as I could.

Twig made a wailing sound. His eyes began to leak fluid, a clear fluid that ran down his face and left trails across his skin.

"What . . . what are you doing?"

I reached out to touch his face, but he turned away, holding up a gripper as if to push me back. He flopped down onto one of the benches, and hid his eyes in his grippers.

"Twig. Twig-la. Let me look. Are you hurt?" I gently pulled his grippers away from his face. Could he be bleeding? Blood was thick and dark blue. This looked more like water.

He made a loud snuffling noise. I couldn't see any injuries to his eyes, although they were so small, it was hard to see anything. I bent closer and touched the wetness. These animals . . . these people . . . seemed always to be losing water, wasting water.

He snuffled again, and wiped at the wetness. He spoke, his voice muffled and flat. Then he wiggled off the bench. He went to the back of the star and opened a door set in the wall. I thought it was a way out, that he was leaving, and I started to follow, but the door led to another, much smaller room. Discarded skins hung from the walls, like the one he had molted while Cheko and I watched. And I knew I had been right. It *was* more like Grandmother's cloak than skin.

Twig pulled a pouchlike bag off a hook. He closed

the door and filled the bag from a shelf nearby. Filled it with small clear objects in many colors. They reminded me of a tislit's float sacs, and I closed my nostrils, even though the smell here was already bad enough.

When the bag was full, Twig turned to me. He made a soft sound by pushing air out past his almost-closed lips. I thought I had never heard such a sad sound. Then he climbed out of the star.

I was glad to walk away from the smell and the star's cold deadness. Twig led the way to the path. As we stepped out onto its open surface, something rustled in the underbrush. Twig squeaked. His gripper slid into mine. An elma scurried across the path, followed quickly by his hatchlings. Twig pressed closer to me. I was reminded of Cheko, before her second molting, when she had been smaller and not so sure of herself. "See," I said. "It's nothing to be afraid of." But Twig left his gripper in mine all the way back to the molting cave, and I didn't try to remove it.

He set his bag in the shade near the mouth of the cave. He took out one of the sacs, snipped the end off with his teeth and sucked up the contents, making funny little smacking noises. Then he dug out another one, opened it and held it up to me.

"Food?" I asked, and he blinked. I took the swollen sac, and it squished a little under my digits. It was rude not to accept food. And Twig was looking at me, his eyes bright and expectant, as he had looked at me in the star.

I held the sac above my mouth, and I squeezed. The food slid into my mouth, in one big, slimy glob. I had never tasted anything so awful. I swallowed hard and fast.

Twig showed me his teeth. "Thank you," I managed to say. "It was . . . interesting." And I took the water jug and drank deeply.

Twig bent and picked up the end of the lisla creeper. He tied it carefully back around his leg. Then he looked up at me and showed me his teeth again.

Not an animal. Not an Outsider. Certainly not Family. What else could he be? My mind was as empty as a shatalsha in the Season of Bare Branches. And I thought I should be frightened, but I wasn't.

"I really have to go now. They'll be angry," I said. I reached out and rubbed my gripper across his mossy head. It was softer than I expected. "I'll be back, Twig-la," I said. "I'll be back as soon as I can."

8
Season of Harvest

I slept badly that night. Images of Outsiders and star hatchlings swam in the sleeping tank with me, pushing for space with Shefa and Shelum. I was glad to feel Uncle Hasa's claw rapping on my head, glad to blow the water out of my gills and climb out to join the Family at the Basking.

I went to the molting cave after the first meal, telling Father that Uncle Hamsha had told me to go to the river and check the nets. I knew Twig had his own food, but I wasn't sure about water. And I wanted to see him again. We sat for a while outside the cave, and I tried to teach him to play Next Line by the rules. But after several games, he rubbed out my drawings and crawled into the cave and wouldn't come out again.

When I returned to the Clearing, I found the Family gathered around Grandmother in front of the food house.

"Five eggs, Shem," Shelum told me as I came up beside him. His tongue unrolled so far I wondered if he would be able to get it back in. "And Grandmother thinks they're all healthy."

"That's good news, Shelum," I said, and I meant it. I craned my head over those around me. "Did Cheko come back with Grandmother?"

"Cheko is basking," Father answered me as he passed us on his way to the food house. "Leave her alone." He clicked a claw. "And I don't know what you were thinking of yesterday, Shem. Those hatchling tanks aren't scrubbed."

As soon as Shelum was hard at work on the tanks, I went to find Cheko.

She was stretched out on the basking rock, the lasha draped across her chest. She didn't even open her eyes when I told her the star hatchling could talk. "Your brain is starting to rot, Shem," she said lazily.

I wanted to shake her, shake her so hard the lasha would go flying, but I managed to keep my grippers tight against my sides. "He talked to me, Cheko. I know he did. And he told me his name."

"Of course he did, Shem. And what is his name?"

"Twig. His name is Twig."

Cheko laughed so loudly the lasha awoke. Cheko opened her eyes, too, and looked at me. "Twig! What kind of name is that?"

"I . . . I don't know. But he showed me a twig and

he pointed to himself and what else can that mean, Cheko?"

Cheko laughed again. "Oh, Shem. I wish I had been there. I wish I could have watched the two of you. I suppose you told him your name, too?"

"Well . . ."

"You did! Oh, Shem. I can't believe you wasted time trying to talk to a stupid animal."

"He's not stupid, Cheko. And . . . and he's not an animal."

Cheko sat up. "Shem, making noises isn't the same as talking. This lasha makes noises, but you don't think she's trying to tell you anything, do you?"

The lasha raised its head and beeped. Its little tongue flicked in and out, almost as if it were smiling.

Cheko *did* smile. "See, Shem. Do you think she was telling you her name?"

Standing there, far from the molting cave and Twig, I felt a small sprout of doubt push up into my mind. "It was different," I said, but my voice sounded uncertain, even in my own flaps. I bent closer to Cheko. "He shared food with me," I whispered.

Seeing her gills flare pleased me. "I don't believe it," she said.

"He picked up a tislit," I said, "and he broke it into two pieces, and he gave me the bigger piece!"

But she only smiled again. "That just shows how

dumb he really is, Shem. The lasha would have taken the whole thing and run away with it."

"He shared *his* food, too," I said. "The food he got from the star."

"What?" She sat up, and pushed the lasha off, paying no attention as it bounced to the ground. Her neck and her gill pouches colored with her anger.

I moved back a step. "I took him to the star, Cheko."

She pinched my gill pouch with her claw. "How could you do such a stupid thing, Shem? He might have gotten away!"

"He was going to go by himself. If I hadn't gone with him, he could have ended up lost in the forest."

"You still shouldn't have done it. Not without asking me first." She gave my pouch an extra pinch, then let go. "What did you do at the star?"

I rubbed my pouch. "We went inside."

"Both of you?"

I blinked.

"Well? What was it like?"

"It was . . . small," I said. "And strange."

Cheko hissed. "That's it? Small and strange?"

I stared down at my digits, rubbing back and forth along the tops of my claws. "It wasn't anything like an egg. There were benches, Cheko."

"Benches?"

"With backs. To sit in, I think."

"Benches," Cheko said again, and I could tell this had made her stop and think.

"There were lots of benches."

Cheko stared at me.

"Maybe there are more." I put my grippers on her claws. "Maybe his Family is wandering around the forest, looking for him. And he must be missing them, must be missing his Family."

She jerked her claws away and gestured with her gripper toward the Clearing. "They wouldn't be anything like us, Shem. They wouldn't be a Family." She poked me with her claw tip. "Anyway, you don't even know for sure those were benches. You said everything was strange. Right?"

"Well. Right."

"That explains it. You're getting all excited about nothing." She clucked, and the lasha came slinking back. "What did the food taste like?"

Awful, I thought. "Different," I said.

She stretched out again on the warm rock. "You should be more careful, Shem. Now go away. I'm tired. Eggs are very tiring."

I watched her wiggle into a comfortable position. Then I left her to her thoughts and went back to my work.

In the food house, I covered my grippers with elma skins and helped Uncle Hasa toss the hot rocks into the stone cauldron of water. As the water began to heat up, the air in the food house became warm and misty. I opened my gills a little to catch the moisture.

"If the Great Shatalsha brought forth one fruit," I said slowly, "and all our people are on it, can there be other people? Can the Great Shatalsha have other fruit with other people?"

Uncle Hasa dropped another rock into the pot. He stared at me. Then he hissed. "Keep your mind on your grippers and your grippers on your work, Shem," he said.

The water was bubbling when Father came into the food house. "Your grandmother would speak to us all," he said.

Grandmother waited until we were assembled in front of the sleeping house. Then she raised her grippers. "I have spoken with a shatalsha," she said. "The Season of Harvest has begun!"

"No more yalas!" Shelum said.

"Shatalsha juice," Shefa said.

"And harvesting," I said. I was allowed to help for the first time during the last Season of Harvest, climbing behind Father in his shatalsha. I had loved being up so far above the forest floor, feeling the broad leaves around me like a protective curtain. I had loved plucking the ripe, firm fruit and filling our picking bags until they could hold no more. Father, I remembered, had sung while he picked.

The next morning was full of the haste and excitement of harvest preparations. I went to the food house to help Father and Uncle Hasa distribute the picking bags and the harnesses. It soon became clear that we had more bags than grippers.

"The problem," Uncle Hasa said, "will be Silef's shatalsha. Since he's gone . . ."

"May his spirit bloom forever," Father said.

"Yes, yes," Uncle Hasa said. "But since he's gone, his shatalsha is untended. We can't leave the fruit to wither on the branches."

"Let me do it, Father," I said.

"You, Shem?" Uncle Hasa's tongue flicked, just a little.

"I know I can do it. Last year you said I could pick almost as well as a Grown One."

"But you've never been up alone, Shem," Father said. "And Shefa and Shelum aren't ready to climb."

"Cheko will go with him."

We all turned, startled. Grandmother stood in the doorway of the food house, Cheko at her side. Cheko's crest was drooping.

"Cheko?" Father and Uncle Hasa exchanged glances.

"We have lost too many. In times of need, every gripper must work for the Family. I will return to the Nesting Place, and Cheko will remain to help." Grandmother gave Cheko a little push. "She is more than able to climb. She is pleased to go with Shem up the shatalsha."

"Yes, Grandmother," Father and Uncle Hasa said together. And they began to outfit us both with harnesses and picking bags.

When we were finally ready, we left the food house for the picking path. I saw that Cheko's crest was again high and her steps were quick.

"You seem awfully eager to do flathead work," I said, hurrying to keep up.

"That's because I'm not going to do it."

"You have to, Cheko. You heard Grandmother. We need every gripper."

"Not my grippers." Cheko walked faster, and when we came to the fork in the path, she turned toward the molting cave.

9
Up a Tree

I was sitting in my usual place just inside the mouth of my cave, watching the sun work its way across the clearing. Yesterday Little Claws had shown up when the sun had just reached the big lump on the side of the fallen tree trunk. All he'd wanted to do was draw pictures in the dirt. At first, I'd thought he was trying to tell me something, and I'd gotten excited. But he'd drawn really slowly, one little line at a time. And when he was done, I couldn't figure out what it was supposed to be. After about the third picture, I don't know why, but Little Claws started to remind me of Jeffrey—Jeffrey when he'd bug me and bug me to play some dumb game with a lot of rules I didn't understand. I'd gone back into the cave. It wasn't good for me to be out in the UV.

Now, even though I was sitting in the shade, I was sweating. Sweat is so disgusting. I mean, it's okay when you're in the gym and you're supposed to sweat, but I knew it couldn't be good to just sweat when you're sitting around doing nothing. I wondered what Dad, old Mr. Adventure, thought about it. He hated to sweat. He was always trying to get out of gym time. "Serves you right, Dad," I shouted as loud as I could. Something squawked in the bushes.

I checked the transponder again. Still nothing. What was taking them so long? Were they even trying to find me? Were they just going to leave me here on this strange planet with trees and bad air and Indigies with claws? I took a deep breath, to keep from crying, and of course that made me feel dizzy and awful. I flopped down flat on my back and bruised my shoulder on a rock. "Think, Hanna," I said. "Think like Andrea Hadaka. What would Andrea Hadaka do in this situation?"

If the problem was that I was out of range of the other Terrans, then I needed to move. I couldn't just wait around and go crazy. I needed to get in their range. I sat up and looked out at all the trees and bushes. I'd seen a comdisc one time about this place on Terra called Oregon. There'd been trees there, too, but nothing like this. I couldn't just start wandering around. I knew I'd get lost before I'd gone half a meter. I didn't even think I could find my way back to the pod by myself.

I needed Little Claws to help me. I scrubbed at the sides of my head. If I couldn't make Little Claws work the radio in the pod, how was I ever going to bring him online about transponders?

The bushes rustled, and Little Claws walked into the clearing. I stood up and smiled. "Hi," I said. And then Big Claws walked up behind him. That stopped me. For some reason I'd thought Little Claws would be alone from now on. I forced myself to step out of the cave. Just don't look at his claws, Hanna, I told myself. And keep smiling.

Little Claws said something. He came close and put his hand on my chest and made the sound that I think is him trying to say "Hanna."

"Right," I said. And I tried to make that slippery shushing noise that's the closest I get to his name.

He looked over his shoulder. Big Claws was staring at us. The fan things were sticking out from the sides of his neck. Little Claws said something to him, and Big Claws hissed an answer.

"Look," I said. This part shouldn't be too hard. "I need to go . . . I mean, to walk . . ."—and I walked a little bit to show them—"away from here." I waved my hand around at the clearing. I pointed to the transponder. "This will help me find my family." And I thought maybe I could draw a picture of them. Maybe a picture would help. But Big Claws was saying something, and Little Claws started untying the vine from around my ankle. "Oh, oh yeah. That's great." And I thought, maybe they're not so dumb.

When both ends of the vine were free, Little Claws coiled it around one of his arms. He was talking, and Big Claws sounded mad when he answered. He pushed at me, shoving me toward the bushes. "Wait. Wait." I dashed into the cave and grabbed my pack. No telling how far we'd have to go. "Okay," I said, and I led the way through the bushes. "You guys are amazing. You came on-line immediately!"

On the path, I walked behind Big Claws and in front of Little Claws. I had to watch out for Big Claws' tail. Just when I'd worked out how to walk beside it, it would twitch, and I'd have to jump over it. I really didn't want to step on it.

When we got to the wider path, we turned right. I was sure we had turned left before, on our way to the pod. "Good," I said, and I pulled out the transponder. "Trying another direction is good." Little Claws reached out and rubbed my head. I had to jump to miss Big Claws' tail.

We were walking fast. Sweat poured down my face and soaked my shirt. Even my feet were sweating, inside my thin deck shoes. My lungs started to ache, the air burning down inside them. I tried to take shallower breaths, but it didn't really help. Even though the transponder was still blank, I was glad when Little Claws said something, and Big Claws suddenly stopped. I dropped my pack on the ground and tried to catch my breath.

We were standing just a couple of meters off the path. There was a big huge box-thing on rollers. It was next to the biggest tree I have ever seen. I had to tip my head way back to see up into the branches. "Wow," I said, when I could talk again. "This is some tree."

Little Claws and Big Claws were looking up, too, like they were maybe thinking the same thing.

Then Big Claws pointed at the box and said something. And then he pointed at me, and then up, up the trunk to where the first branch grew.

"Oh, no," I said. "No. We don't have to go higher. I mean, I think the transponder works just as well on the ground."

They weren't listening to me. Little Claws went up the trunk, scaling right up it, using the pointy things on his claws and his toes. He tied the vine to the branch, and the free end slithered down to the ground. Big Claws gave the vine a couple of hard tugs. Then he held it out to me.

I shook my head. "You're crazy," I said. "I mean, I really appreciate what you guys are trying to do, but, well, I'm not going to climb up that tree."

Big Claws stepped closer to me. He said something, slowly and loudly, like I was aurally challenged. Then he stuck out his claw and nipped the skin just under my chin. "Ouch!" Big Claws pulled. "Okay, okay." I clipped the transponder onto my belt and grabbed the vine.

It was just like climbing the ropes in the gym on the *Turing*. I wished Dr. Cynthia Wu could see me now. I wished Andrea could see me now. I did a lot better with somebody right behind me, snapping at me with big, sharp claws.

Panting hard, I clambered onto the branch and stood up. I had to duck my head to keep from hitting it on the next higher branch. I looked around, at Little Claws, flicking his tongue out in little short breaths, at the smaller branches, covered in some kind of fruit, at the wide, thick, glossy leaves, and at the ground, way, way down below us. The ground sort of swooped and swirled. I dropped facedown on the branch, wrapping my arms as far around it as I could, digging my fingernails into the soft, spongy bark and clamping my eyes tight shut.

I heard Big Claws climb up beside me, heard them talking. And then, after a while, I felt Little Claws' rubbery fingers on my right hand. He pried it gently up off the branch and slid something over it and along my arm. Then he did the same thing to my other hand.

I forced my eyes open. I stared at the bark, greenish blue and tracked with grooves. Slowly, I lifted my head. The ground was still really far away, but it didn't spin anymore. I sat up. Little Claws had fastened some kind of harness-thing to me. A long vine ran from the back to one of the smaller branches.

Big Claws came over and gave me a poke with his claw. He pointed to Little Claws, standing about a meter away. Little Claws was picking the fat, purple fruit, dropping it into a bag hung over his shoulder. Big Claws held another bag out to me.

I looked at him. "You brought me all the way up here to pick fruit? Don't you guys have mobicoms to do stuff like this?"

His claw reached out toward my chin. I got up. "I'm picking," I said. "I'm picking."

I baby-stepped my way over to Little Claws. Big Claws had been wearing a harness like mine, but Little Claws didn't have one. He did have the end of his tail snagged around a small branch.

I checked the transponder. The screen was still blank. Climbing up hadn't helped. I had been right. But the Indigies hadn't been helping me. They'd been bringing me here to pick fruit. Dumb Hanna, I thought. "Dumb Indigies," I said out loud.

Little Claws looked at me. Then, using big, exaggerated movements, he picked a fruit and dropped it into his bag. He said something, and pointed in the bag, and looked at me again. I accessed the way he'd looked at me in the pod, after he'd banged on the com and I'd started crying, and I felt sort of bad. He was doing the best he could.

"Okay," I said. "It's probably better than sitting in the cave all by myself." And I moved over by him and started picking. Little Claws watched me for a minute, then he got to work, too, his tongue flicking.

I almost felt like panting, too. It was hot up in the tree, even though the big, palm-shaped leaves gave lots of shade. The fruit was easy to find. It grew all around us, the bright color showing up clearly among the dark leaves. The work actually wasn't too bad, especially after my stomach stopped churning and the bottoms of my feet stopped tingling.

When our bags were full, Little Claws untied the vine I had climbed up and gave me the free end. He climbed down the trunk, and I lowered the bags on the vine, so he could dump the fruit into the big box. Big Claws roosted on the first branch, but he didn't offer to help. Sitting there like that, watching us, he sort of reminded me of Dr. Geraldo Wu. For the first time, I wondered how Little Claws and Big Claws were related. And whether or not there were any other Indigies around. And just what they were going to do with all that fruit.

We moved up to higher branches. Little Claws would boost me up, then he'd fasten the end of the vine on my harness to one of the littler branches. I hoped it was a really strong vine.

We were probably on our fifth branch when Big Claws called up to us, and we climbed back down to where he was sitting.

Little Claws showed me how to sort of wedge myself between two of the smaller branches. He sat down beside me, and Big Claws sat down on my other side, which made me a little nervous. I don't know why, but I kept thinking maybe Big Claws didn't like me so much. Big Claws took a piece of fruit out of my bag and started eating.

Lunch! I was starving. And my pack was all the way back down on the ground. I started to get up, started to try to explain, but Little Claws put a hand on my knee. He took a piece of fruit, slit the hard outer rind with his claw tip and offered it to me. The inside of the fruit was a light yellow color. I thought I'd take a small bite and then spit it out when they weren't looking. I nibbled an edge. The fruit was soft and squishy and tasted wonderful, sort of like oranges, raspberries, and fireflower melon all rolled together. I swallowed the piece, and I took another big bite, letting the sweet juice fill my mouth and slide down my throat. Some of the juice dripped down my chin. I wiped it with my hand, and then I licked my fingers. "That was great," I said when I'd eaten the whole piece of fruit. I looked at the empty rind. "I hope it doesn't kill me."

And then I heard the voices. Far below us, on the ground. Big Claws hissed and crouched down. And Little Claws reached over and clamped his hand hard over my mouth.

10
Abomination

"Quiet!" Cheko hunched on the branch. She peered down at the forest floor, her eyes and flaps opened to their fullest.

I pushed Twig back into a clump of leaves. His pale skin stood out like a sheemo in a food house. I crouched beside Cheko, straining my ears and my eyes. "Is it Father?" I whispered. "Is it Uncle Hasa?" All I could see were the tops of the mehtas and the bin of ripe fruit, directly below us. The forest was silent again.

Behind us, Twig made a noise, and we both shushed him.

And then I heard the voices, louder and clearer. My digits dug deep into Cheko's shoulder. It wasn't Father and it wasn't Uncle Hasa.

Outsiders!

They came walking along the path, along our path, as if they owned the very forest.

"Are they Council messengers?" I whispered.

Cheko twitched under my gripper. "Too many of them."

The Outsiders were almost directly below us. There *were* too many of them. At least six.

Keep moving, I thought. Keep going. Don't stop here.

But they did stop. One of them had spotted the bin.

"See. We must be near their Clearing." She was an Old One, her crest mottled and her voice deep. She approached the bin and looked inside. "They will have a good harvest, I think," she said.

"They're after our fruit, Shem." Cheko's claws were half-open, and her mouth opened to show her teeth. Color flooded up her neck and across her face. "They've come to steal our fruit."

She frightened me, her cresthead instincts to fight and to kill so clear on her. But she was only one, and they were many.

"I have to stop them," she said.

She stood, and I stood, too, blocking her way. "Wait. Cheko—"

"Move, flathead." She shoved at me with her grippers. My toe talons scratched and scrabbled on the shatalsha's bark. My foot slipped and hit the lisla creeper, still coiled where Twig and I had untied it and left it. The whole thing slid off the branch and plopped into the picking bin.

Below us, claws clicked. "Someone's up there," one

of the Outsiders said. They were all looking up, claws opened, teeth displayed.

Uncle Simla's stories of the horrors and the tragedies before the setting of the Territories flooded into my memory. They would tear Cheko to pieces before my eyes. And Twig? What would they do to Twig?

One of the Outsiders, a younger cresthead, with a tall, waxed crest, stepped to the trunk. "I'm going to see what's up there," she said.

"Good," Cheko whispered, "Good. Come on up."

I didn't say anything. I looked at the cresthead, climbing nearer and nearer. I looked down at the ripe shatalsha, half-filling the bin. And I stepped off the branch.

I thought I heard them whispering. The harsh accents of the Outsiders and Twig's hoarse croaking. Then the water washed over me, rocking me gently in its liquid arms. I turned and stretched, and a great pain clutched my entire body and would not let it go. I held myself as still as I could, as if I were a hatchling again. As if I had no arms and no legs, no claws and no digits, nothing that could hurt so much.

"Shem-la. Shem-la. It's time to come out."

A gripper pushed at me, and I bobbed in the warm waters. I raised my lids, very carefully. Father was leaning over the edge of the tank, looking in at me.

"Is it morning already? Is it time for the Basking?"

"It is morning. But no one has basked today."

I blew water from my gills and hoisted myself out of the tank. Father ran gentle digits over my arms. "Only some bruises and a new tailtip. You're lucky, Shem. Lucky you landed in the bin and not on the ground. Lucky the fruit was ripe and soft." He paused, then added, grudgingly, "And lucky the Outsiders carried you home."

And I remembered. "Cheko? Where is Cheko?"

Father held up his gripper. "She's fine. She's here."

"But, Father. Outsiders . . ." I said.

"They're here, too." He made a face, as if he had found rotten yalas at the bottom of a basket.

I peered around the door frame. The Outsiders sat in two groups near the edge of the Clearing. The uncles clustered in the door of the food house, watching them. Shefa and Shelum and Cheko peeked out of the food-house window.

I looked at Father. "Why are they here?"

He tipped the tank to drain. "They won't tell us anything. They're waiting for the crestheads. And there's no telling when they'll be back." His tail twitched. I had never seen Father look frightened before.

I helped him wipe out the tank. "What about the shatalsha?" I asked, wondering, What about Twig? Where was Twig? "Has anyone gone to pick my shatalsha?"

"No one has done anything but stand around and watch the Outsiders." He looked at me. "We will have much work to do, when they leave. Today's work and yesterday's and tomorrow's as well, no doubt. So rest while you can, Shem-la." He rubbed my head. "We'll need your grippers soon enough. Now go to the food house. We're keeping everyone safe there."

Cheko shoved her lasha into a surprised Shelum's arms and made room for me beside her at the window. "Are you all right? I couldn't believe it when you just jumped out of the shatalsha, like you thought you were a mechaka."

I leaned closer to her. "What about Twig?" I whispered. "Where is he?"

She glanced over at Shelum and Shefa. They had eyes and flaps only for the Outsiders. "He's still up in the shatalsha. I think."

"You think?"

"I haven't been able to get away, Shem. Father won't let anyone leave the Clearing while they're here. We can't even leave the food house! All because of those Outsiders." And she clicked her claws in their direction.

They clustered near the entrance to the picking path. My flaps could barely catch their voices, low and hoarse.

"Two families," Cheko whispered. "Together."

My tail touched my ankles and hugged them. Two different families of Outsiders, traveling together. Something truly terrible must have happened.

The sun had just reached the midmorning branch when Father slipped into the crowded food house.

"They are back at last," he said. "You must all come out and greet them."

Grandmother came around the sleeping house first. She carried a hatchling basket in her grippers. A little murmur of relief and excitement came from the uncles. We had almost forgotten about the eggs. "Only one?" someone whispered, but he was quickly silenced.

As each aunt rounded the sleeping house and saw the Outsiders, her gills flared and her claws opened. But Grandmother gave no sign that anything was out of the ordinary. She held the basket high. "Our hatchling," she said. "A cresthead," she added, more loudly.

Mother came forward and took the basket. We followed her to the hatchling tank set up close by the door to the sleeping house, and watched as she tipped the hatchling into the warm waters. "Welcome, Daughter," she said, and we all echoed, "Welcome."

The aunts had formed a line between us and the Outsiders, who had drawn closer, stretching and craning, trying to see over our heads. I looked at Grandmother and my mother, but their gills were flat, their claws were closed. As if Outsiders were a common sight in our Clearing. Or as if they had expected them.

Grandmother turned, slowly, and two of the aunts opened a pathway for her. "Greetings, Outsiders," she said.

"Greetings, Outsider." The two Old Ones answered as one. They wore their Council cloaks now, and Grandmother looked smaller beside them.

"We would know," Grandmother said, and her voice was not small, "why you have entered our Clearing."

"We bring a call . . ." began one, but the other interrupted her. "It has been many seasons since we have seen a hatchling," she said, and her voice was hoarse and low. "We ask that we might look."

There was an angry murmur from the aunts and gasps from the uncles, but Grandmother extended her grippers and motioned toward the tank. "See our joy."

Like young sheels before a skiff, we parted and made room for the Outsiders. Mother moved last.

The Outsiders watched the hatchling in silence. After a moment, Grandmother came forward, moving them back and away. "Now you must tell us why you have come to our Clearing."

The Old One with the mottled crest glanced around at us. She looked at the other Old One, who blinked. "Messengers have been sent to all the families throughout the forest." She paused, as though waiting to be sure that Grandmother was listening. "We are issuing a call to a special Council."

"We must discuss a grave matter," the other Old One said. "A matter that concerns the entire forest," and she moved her gripper, as if to indicate all of us and the mehtas and talfas as well.

Cheko's digits dug into the scales on my arm.

"We are ready to leave at once," Grandmother said, and Mother and Aunt Kichel blinked. And again it seemed as if they had been expecting this. They hurried toward the sleeping house, to get their Council cloaks, and I saw Father and Uncle Hasa hurrying toward the food house. They would have to prepare food and water for the journey and the Council time.

The Outsiders had moved toward the path, separating again into their two groups. The uncles and aunts still stood around the hatchling tank, and I moved over to join them, but Cheko stopped me. She put a digit to her lips and pulled me over into the shade of the food house, near one of the groups of Outsiders.

They didn't pay any attention to us. They were arguing, in quiet, tense voices.

"I say this is *not* a matter for the Council," one of them said. "Such a thing is not for discussion." She clicked, once, and Cheko's grip tightened on my arm. The Old One of the family closed her flaps and sighed.

"It's an abomination, Grandmother," another one said. "An absolute abomination."

Cheko's digits pinched my arm. "It's Twig," she whispered, close to my flap. "They're talking about Twig." Her tail slapped against my leg. "Well, I won't let them have him." And she pushed right between the Outsiders and ran for the picking path. And I ran after her.

11
"They *Are* Here!"

You don't dream at all in stasis. Everything is too slowed down. Even your brain. That's what Dr. Geraldo Wu told us. But your brain makes up for those missed dreams. When you're out of stasis, your "real sleep" dreams get very, very intense.

I was having one of those dreams, and I knew it was a dream, but I didn't want to wake up. Mom and Jeffrey were there with me. They were talking, telling me about what they'd been doing. Jeffrey told a joke, one of his dumb jokes, and we were laughing, and then Mom clicked her claws.

I jerked awake. I was wedged tight between a branch and the trunk of the tree. It was pitch black all around me. There had been three moons, a small one up high and a big one with a small satellite moon lower down. But they must have set already. I could feel the wind, and it blew the leaves above me, opening spaces that let me see the stars.

Why had Little Claws jumped out of the tree? Big Claws had turned away, and he had made this really horrible, loud noise. Then he had taken off down the trunk, headfirst, as fast as he could go. I had been afraid to look, afraid of what I'd see. There'd been a lot of yelling, and then, when I had dared to look, Little Claws and Big Claws had disappeared.

I hoped Little Claws was okay. But why did they have to take the vine with them? Why did they have to leave me stuck up here in this stupid tree?

I dug around in the bag and pulled out a fruit. I took a bite of the hard rind and spat it out, quick. I wished I had a knife. Or claws. I took a small bite of the insides. It didn't taste quite as good as it had that first time. I dropped it back in the bag.

I held the transponder up in front of my face, thinking how neat it would be to all of a sudden have the screen light up in the dark. But nothing happened.

And then I heard the voice again. Not down on the ground, but up there in the tree with me. It almost sounded like branches rubbing together, and that's what I'd told myself it was. Except it sort of sounded like someone talking, too. Like someone with a funny, deep, creaky voice trying to tell me something. "It's probably just another dream, Hanna," I whispered. "Just a bad dream." And I huddled down in my nest of leaves and wished the sun would come up.

When I woke up again, the sun was high in the sky. I couldn't tell if it was morning or afternoon. I sat up and stretched. I had a plan. I was better at thinking up plans than I had expected, and I wished somebody was there with me so I could show off a little bit. Seeing as how I couldn't climb down, not without the vine, I was going to climb up, higher even than I'd gone with Little Claws. I figured I should be able to see out, over some of the forest. My pod had knocked down trees and bushes when it had landed. I'd seen that when I'd gone back with Little Claws. So other pods would have done the same thing. Maybe I could see which way those other pods had gone. Where they had landed. And then, well, then, I'd just have to figure out some way to get down out of this tree.

I took off the harness, because the vine was just going to get in my way. Climbing up wasn't hard, but I had to stop often and catch my breath. When I thought I was probably high enough, I sat down and scooted my way closer to the end of the branch. I pushed the leaves aside and looked out. It reminded me of the reality disc that lets you climb to the top of the cliffs on Ravenna Prime and look out over the Sea of Sighs. Only, instead of water, I was looking out at a sea of leaves, a sea that moved and shifted with the wind. Maybe four hundred meters away, another big tree like mine stuck up like a beacon. It was really amazing. And I thought how much

Mom and Dad must both be loving this. A real adventure.

I couldn't see anything that looked like the place where an escape pod might have landed. Not even my own pod. All I could see were leaves and branches. It was so empty and dead-looking. There weren't any vehicles. No towers of cities. No solar catchers or windmills. Maybe the Indigies had built their cities underground, like on Honolulu Too. Except Little Claws and Big Claws had been above ground. Trying to figure out the Indigies made my head ache.

I climbed back down to the first branch. I ate another fruit. I tried to think of another plan. I tried to think what Andrea Hadaka would do if she were up this tree.

Something scrabbled and scratched on the trunk below me. I scrunched down among the leaves. It might be one of those big ugly animals with scaly wings I'd seen flying around.

Little Claws climbed up beside me.

It was almost as good as seeing Mom or Dad or even Jeffrey. I wrapped both my arms around him and gave him a big hug. His funny, damp smell filled my nose, but I didn't care. He rubbed my head, and it was okay this time.

Then Big Claws climbed up on the branch, carrying the vine over his shoulder. And I was glad to see him, too. But I didn't hug him.

I let go of Little Claws and took a step back. "I thought you were dead," I said. I tapped him on the chest and pointed down at the ground and covered my eyes, then uncovered them. "I'm glad you're okay."

Little Claws said something, and Big Claws answered. Then they looked at me, like I was supposed to say something, too. "We aren't going to pick fruit again, are we?"

And then they started arguing with each other, or it sounded like arguing, fast words and loud voices. Except, after a few minutes, Little Claws was the only one talking.

Big Claws was just standing there, with his mouth dropped open and his eyes bugged out, and everything sticking out from the sides of his head. He looked just like Jeffrey when he's pretending to be totally amazed. I had to laugh. Even Little Claws noticed it, because he stopped talking. He gave Big Claws a poke, and Big Claws still didn't move or speak.

Little Claws looked at me. I shrugged. "Maybe he's sick or something."

Big Claws moved so suddenly we both jumped, and if Little Claws hadn't grabbed me, I probably would have fallen right out of the tree. Big Claws dropped the vine and tied it back onto the branch. He looked at me and pointed down at the ground.

He didn't have to tell me twice. I slid down so fast the vine burned the palms of my hands. I grabbed my pack, and Big Claws had me by the arm, and he was pulling me down the path as fast as he could. Little Claws was close behind us.

"Where are we going?" I said. "Is something wrong?" And I had an awful sinking feeling. Maybe Big Claws had completely downloaded, up there in the tree. "Where are you taking me now?" I tried to pull back, to pull away, but Big Claws just tightened his grip on my sleeve, and we were running down the path.

After a few meters, all I could think about was getting my breath. Running was not a good idea at all. My lungs ached with the effort of trying to get enough oxygen. I had to slow down, but Big Claws kept pulling me along, dragging me along. The pain in my chest got sharper and sharper. I didn't care where we were going or what I was going to have to do. All I wanted was one good, full breath.

We stopped and I didn't care why. I sat down, right in the middle of the path, right next to Big Claws' feet, and I hung my head down, and I breathed, very slowly and carefully and painfully.

Finally it stopped hurting. Little Claws and Big Claws were both standing there, looking down at me. Little Claws said something and bent down, his fingers resting gently on my hair. "Okay," I said. "I'm okay." And I stood up.

Big Claws hissed and sighed. Little Claws pointed along the trail.

"Okay," I said again. "But we really need to slow down. I'll be all right if we just walk."

And it was almost like they were on-line because we did go slower, almost creeping along the path. I realized we were moving downhill now, just a little bit. The path was wider, and the dirt under our feet deeper and softer. Big Claws stopped again, all of a sudden.

I edged past his tail and peeked around his back. We were at a bend in the path. Beyond, it opened onto a wide riverbank. An Indigie was there already, pulling a net made of vines along the sand.

Big Claws shoved me back until I was behind Little Claws. Big Claws whispered, and Little Claws blinked like he had something in both eyes. And then, we went single-file onto the beach. Little Claws kept his hand out, keeping me behind him.

The other Indigie spoke in a loud voice. I couldn't see around Little Claws, but I heard Big Claws answer. Little Claws and I kept moving, sideways, toward the water.

The Indigie said something else, even louder. Little Claws and I kept moving. I stumbled. I'd tripped on the edge of a platform, a dock built out over the water. We stepped up and moved along it. Boats, or things like boats, were tied up on either side. Little Claws stopped next to one on the end.

That's when the transponder started beeping.

I jerked it off my belt. The screen was lit up and visuals flashed across it. "They *are* here!" I shouted. I stepped up beside Little Claws. "See!" And I held the transponder up.

They were all staring at me. All three of them. And they were very, very quiet. I held the transponder up higher, and the beeping got a little louder. "See?" I said again.

The other Indigie peeked around Big Claws' shoulder. We looked at each other for a minute.

"Uh . . . hi," I said, and I gave a little wave.

He shrieked, a really amazingly loud shriek. Big Claws shoved him, hard. Then Big Claws ran toward us, shouting something and waving his hands and his claws.

Little Claws picked me up and tossed me into the boat. Big Claws tumbled in after me. Little Claws untied the vine that held the boat to the platform. He jumped in, picked up a pole lying in the bottom and pushed us away.

The transponder beeped stronger and louder. The locator arrow began to flash. "I'm on my way," I said. "We're coming to meet you." All three of us.

12
Out of the Territory

The current grabbed us. The skiff rocked, and water splashed over the side. Cheko sat down abruptly on a pile of nets. I balanced in the stern. Desperately trying to remember everything that Uncle Hamsha had taught me, I pushed the talfa pole into the sandy riverbed, forcing the skiff to straighten and steady, forcing us into the slower water closer to the riverbank.

I looked up and saw that Twig was standing in the bow with the other pole. He pushed with me, matching my strokes, the long dark moss swinging back and forth across his shoulders. He straightened, glanced back at me, and showed me his teeth.

I looked back at the dock. Shefa had disappeared. I could imagine what he was doing now, could imagine him running to the Clearing, running to tell everyone that Shem and Cheko were . . . were . . . I rested my pole against the side of the skiff. "Just what are we doing, Cheko?"

Her eyes had that strange inward look that they'd had up in the shatalsha. "We're taking Twig to the Council Clearing."

I nearly dropped the pole. "To the Council Clearing? Cheko! That's stupid! The Outsiders will be there." And Grandmother. I didn't know which was worse.

"The shatalsha said that's what we should do."

I eased the skiff around the humped back of a sandbank. "You heard the voice of the shatalsha?" I said when we were safely on the other side. "I didn't know you could do that."

"I didn't know I could, either." She opened and closed her flaps. "There I was, listening to you tell me all about why we couldn't take Twig back to the Clearing. And then all of a sudden, there were all these other voices. Talking all at once, but all together." She wrapped her tail around her feet. "Creaky voices. As if branches could rub together and make words."

I looked out across the water, the sun just starting to glint on its surface. All at once, I was glad I was a flathead, glad I would never have to listen to the voices in the branches. "And they said we should take Twig to the Council Clearing?" My tail twitched a little. How did the shatalsha even know about the Council Clearing?

"They didn't call him 'Twig.'" Cheko was weaving her

digits in and out of the holes of one of the nets. "They called him the New Fruit-picker." Her voice was soft and hesitant, with none of her usual bark. "And they didn't actually say the Council Clearing."

I dug the pole deep and forced the skiff to slow. Twig looked back and pulled his pole out of the water. His skin wrinkled and he said something. "What did they say exactly, Cheko?"

"They said that the New Fruit-picker had no roots in this forest. And they said we should take him to the meeting place."

"What does that mean? A meeting place could be . . ."

She swiveled around and looked straight at me. "The Council Clearing. It has to be the Council Clearing. It's the only place we go to meet when it's important." She shook her claw at me. "And the shatalsha thought this was important."

"But . . . but did they say who he's supposed to meet?"

Cheko clicked her claws now, and she didn't look hesitant or inward anymore. She looked, and sounded, like Mother. "Shem. You don't stand around and ask the shatalsha a lot of questions. When they tell you to go, you go."

In the bow, Twig said something, said my name. He pointed at the box, still beeping like a panicked lasha at his side, and he pointed down the river.

"See," Cheko said. "He wants to go, too."

Ahead, the river flowed around a wide belly of land. Beyond that curve was the rock the sheemos favored for basking, the rock that marked the river boundary of our Territory. "We don't actually know where the Council Clearing is, Cheko."

"We know it's downriver." They were both looking at me, Cheko and Twig.

"Uncle Hamsha says the water gets wilder and deeper farther downriver."

"Uncles say a lot of things, Shem."

We floated around the curve, as if the river itself wanted us to go, too. And there was the sheemo rock, empty and sunless. All the other Territories, all the forest where we did not belong, stretched beyond it.

"I'll say it was all my fault, Shem."

I looked down at her. "And what if Outsiders get us? What if . . ." The words withered on my tongue.

"I'll protect you, Shem. I'm not afraid." She looked so strong and so sure that, for a moment, I almost believed her.

"Just remember," I said, "you're taking the blame." I poled hard and fast, and we slid around the rock and out into the current. In the bow, Twig showed us his teeth. Then he pushed with his pole, and we were out of our Territory.

The skiff was the one the uncles used to catch the biggest tislit, the ones that walked the deepest, coldest parts of the river. It was built for the swift waters, but laden with nets and with us, it took all my strength to keep it under control. I maneuvered us as close to the shore, and to the grippers and claws of angry Outsiders, as I dared.

Cheko made herself a nest in a pile of nets, and she lay back, looking out at the riverbank. Talfas and mehtas slipped past us. "You really can't tell it's not our Territory. I mean, it looks just exactly the same," she said.

I let my tail wrap tight around my legs. "It doesn't feel the same," I said. And for a long time, we traveled in silence, broken only by the splashing of the poles and the beeping of Twig's box.

The sun climbed overhead, and I raised my membranes to protect my eyes from the glare off the water. We rounded more curves in the river than I could count. Twig frequently stopped poling and stood with his head tipped back, taking loud, rasping breaths. Keeping the skiff straight in the current and keeping watch for Outsiders took all my energy and concentration. My muscles ached, and I longed to soak them in the warm water of a sleeping tank.

Cheko stirred and looked up at me. "I'm hungry."

"So am I."

"And I'm bored."

I held my tongue.

"Whose Territory are we in now?"

"I don't know."

She lay back. "How much farther do you suppose it is to the Council Clearing?"

"I don't know," I said again.

"Grandmother and Mother and Aunt Kichel never go for more than two or three days. So it can't be too far. Can it?"

"I really don't know."

In the bow, Twig stopped poling altogether. He turned and said something. Then he sat down, dug in his pouch and sucked up the insides of one of the food sacs. He held one out toward Cheko, and she knocked it away with her claw. "Did you really eat that, Shem?"

"Yes."

"Well, I'll never be that hungry."

Twig rested his head on the side of the skiff, his moss trailing down almost into the water. If I rested, the skiff would roll and turn. I stared out at the far shore, trying to distract my stomach and my muscles. I saw a lasha peering out from under a mehta bush. I hadn't been able to see the opposite shore so clearly when we started out. "The river is narrowing," I said, and Cheko grunted.

We passed what looked like a dock, but a dock that had not been used or tended for many seasons. Tislit nets hung dry and ragged from rotting supports, and the skeleton of a skiff baked on the sand. Cheko looked at me, but neither of us said anything.

The sun reached the highest branch and started its

downward climb, but the light still fell full on the river. The warmth felt good, heating my blood and my very bones. The skin on Twig's face glistened with moisture. He dipped his gripper in the river and splashed water across his face. Cheko shouted as some of the drops splashed on her, and Twig showed his teeth.

I knew the river was definitely getting narrower. I could see the leaves and berries on the mehtas now. The current had become stronger as well, and it took more effort to keep the skiff moving straight ahead. I could feel the strain in my gripper arms, and in my legs as well. The water was foaming and swirling around us, and a loud, deep growling filled my flaps. The bow bounced, and spray shot up and soaked us all. Cheko shrieked, and Twig shouted.

Twig was kneeling, pointing ahead of us, and I knew he must still be shouting, but I couldn't hear him above the roaring. The water pushed my pole aside as if it were a sheel.

We swept around another sharp bend, and suddenly, the bow disappeared in front of me, the skiff tipping as if to stand on its head. Cheko was gripping the side. Her mouth strained open.

We slid over what seemed the very edge of the river. The skiff bounced and bucked, and water drenched us from all sides.

And then Twig screamed, and I heard that clearly. He shifted to one side, as if to get away, and I saw we were heading directly toward an enormous rock jutting out of the water.

I leapt over Cheko and knocked Twig aside. Water flew up over the bow and hit me in the face. I stuck out my pole and braced myself for the impact.

The pole hit the rock, and the whole skiff shuddered. The end struck my chest painfully, but I held on with grippers and claws. I pushed hard, leaning my whole weight out. The pole bent, and I heard it creak, and I prayed that Uncle Hamsha had chosen well, that this talfa had been strong. The pole bent even farther.

But Uncle Hamsha knew his work. The pole held, and slowly, reluctantly, the skiff slid past the rock and into the current beyond.

I was still leaning forward. I fell headfirst into the river.

Cold water filled my nostrils and my mouth before I had time to seal them. I tried to cough, but only managed to pull water into my mouth instead of my gills. The cold froze my blood, and even my thoughts slowed and thickened.

But my feet and lower legs were still dry and warm, were still in the skiff. Twig's soft, fat digits pressed into my ankles. Slowly, painfully, I was dragged back into the skiff. My legs and stomach scraped across the side, my head came back into the warm air, and I lay in the bottom, coughing up water, my grippers still clasping tight to the pole.

Cheko and Twig sat behind me. Twig had hold of my ankles. Cheko had hold of Twig. They were both wet and panting.

"Just stay in the skiff from now on, Shem," Cheko said, and Twig blinked like he agreed.

I sat up, wincing at my bruises. The water had slowed, as if the river was tired, too, by all the noise and excitement. The skiff was turning sideways. I moved carefully back to the stern and straightened the skiff out.

The river was not only slower and quieter. It was wider again as well, almost like the tame river of our Territory. My tail relaxed away from my feet, and I loosened my grip on the pole. It wasn't so bad, now. It was almost nice here.

We drifted into a large patch of vaschas spreading out from the bank and around the curve ahead of us. The huge flat blossoms were opening as the sun climbed down, and the spicy scent was heavy in the air. I filled my nostrils. "Isn't it beautiful here, Cheko?"

She was kneeling, watching the river ahead. Then, suddenly, she forced Twig down with one gripper while she dragged nets up over him with the other.

"What are you—"

"Hush. I heard something. Up ahead."

We rounded the bend. Another dock jutted out onto the river. But this one wasn't rotting. This one wasn't empty.

It was crowded with Outsiders. Angry Outsiders.

13
Many Strong Claws

They were all crestheads. One of them stepped forward to stand alone. She raised her claw, flat toward us, and gestured with her gripper. The meaning was clear.

Cheko clicked her claw, and under the nets, Twig made a muffled, gurgling sound. I hoped he could breathe under there.

"Don't move, Cheko," I whispered. I slid the pole into the water and gave a little push. The skiff eased through the vaschas, closer to the dock.

"What are you doing?" Cheko's voice was tight and low. Her face was colored with her anger, and her claws were opening and closing, opening and closing.

"Just wait," I said. "Don't do anything foolish."

The other Outsiders had arrayed themselves behind the Grown One. My own claws began to open, and I willed them shut.

"Outsiders," the Grown One said. "Greetings." Her

accent was as thick on her tongue as the vaschas on the water. I looked at her companions, waiting for them to respond, and then realized, with a start, that she was talking to *us*.

"Uh . . . greetings." I raised my closed claw and dropped it back down by my side.

Cheko pushed between me and the dock. "I'll do the talking," she said. "Greetings." And the claw she raised was open, the sharp hooks threatening in the sunlight.

"Come closer, Outsiders, that we may know your names and your Family."

"You have no need of our names," Cheko said. "And all you need to know is that our Family is large and powerful, with many strong claws."

There was a stirring among the Outsiders, and I heard claws click. Twig's eyes gleamed through the netting. I dug the pole down and felt it sink into the muddy bottom. I dragged against it, slowing the skiff.

"Shem!" Cheko hissed.

"I can't help it, Cheko." I dragged harder on the pole, and the skiff began to turn in a slow circle.

"Outsiders!" The Grown One took a step closer. Her voice was as sharp as her claws. "Approach the dock that we may know your name and your Family."

We were floating backward now. I looked over my shoulder. "I'm sorry, Grown One. I can't seem to get the skiff under control."

"Flathead," someone said.

And another muttered, "I'd like to give him a gripper. And a claw."

"Stop fooling around, Shem!" Cheko rapped me on the shoulder with her closed claw. "This is serious."

"It is our right to know the name and the Family of all who enter our Territory. The Council declared it as our right when the Territories were first established."

"History lessons," Cheko said.

"And we have had more than our share of Outsiders of late," the Grown One added, as if Cheko had not spoken.

"Turn us around," Cheko said, hitting me with her claw again. "Turn us around so I can talk."

I straightened the skiff with an effort, and we were again heading toward the dock. Cheko stood tall and stiff in the bow. "The Council also decreed that all Families have the right to travel on the river," she said, in a loud, clear voice. "And without having to answer so many questions!"

I plunged the pole into the bottom as hard as I could. The skiff shot forward. Cheko stumbled and sat down, right on Twig. I heard him *oof* softly.

We were heading straight for the dock. Outsiders shouted and leapt for shore. The Grown One gathered herself, as if she were about to jump into the river.

I hurried to the bow, treading on Twig, who *oofed* again. I jammed the pole down into the mud, and the skiff stopped, a gripper's span from the dock.

"Wait, Outsider." The Grown One was the only one left on the dock. She held up her gripper. "Wait. Don't move. Members of our Family will come to help you."

Two crestheads were wading into the river.

Behind me, Cheko was struggling to her feet. "We have the right—" she began again.

"What's that noise?" The Grown One was turning her head from side to side, her flaps open.

Twig's beeping was loud in the sudden silence.

"It's my lasha," Cheko said, even more loudly and clearly. "I have a pet lasha."

"Not a very healthy one," one of the Outsiders said.

"Outsiders!" I shouted. The two crestheads wading closer paused, knee-deep in the river. "Outsiders, my name is Shem. I am of the Family That Lives by the Sheemo Rock." I gave the pole one small, careful push. Just enough to point the bow back toward the open river. "My sister's name is Cheko," I said, and I ducked to avoid her swinging claw. I gave the pole another push. "There are strange happenings in the forest, Grown One."

"And stranger happenings on the river," the Grown One said.

I looked back at the group clustered on the shore. "Our Family has sent us on a mission." I didn't think I should mention the shatalsha. "A mission to the Council."

"Your Family has sent a flathead to the special Council? And a Young One?" The Outsiders swayed with amusement.

"I'm not so young that I can't fight!" Cheko leaned over the side, her grippers outstretched and her claws opened. "Get me closer, Shem, so I can show them how sharp my claws are!"

I pushed again, away from the dock.

"Come ashore," one of the Outsiders shouted. "Come ashore and we will show you claws!" The two crestheads in the water waded closer.

Cheko leaned farther and hissed her fury, and the Outsiders began to hiss in return. I saw Twig burrow farther under the nets.

The situation was getting totally out of gripper. I dug the pole deep and gave a big push.

"No!" Cheko screamed.

I pushed again and felt the first grab of the current. The two crestheads had waded waist deep. Please, O Great Shatalsha, I thought, make the current swift and the Outsiders slow. "Sorry we can't stay!" I shouted over my shoulder.

"Shem, you sheemo brain!" For a moment, I thought that Cheko was going to use her claw on me. But the current had us now. We were floating free, picking up speed. I dug the pole into the mud again and pushed. I could hear shouts of fury from the shore. I set my feet to pull the pole back up for the next push, but it wouldn't move. I pulled harder, thinking it must be stuck, in deep mud, in the last of the vaschas. I looked around to see, and found myself looking right into the eyes of one of the Outsiders.

The other was grabbing the side of the skiff.

Cheko shrieked. I saw the nets jump, and then subside. I ripped the pole out of the Outsider's grippers and brought it down, as hard as I could, across her crest. She disappeared under the water.

The skiff tipped as the other one pulled herself up. Cheko rushed at her, teeth bared, claws opened. The skiff tipped farther. Twig cried out. The Outsider's eyes widened. She lifted herself farther up, looking inside the skiff. But then Cheko's claw sank into her soft gill pouches, and the Outsider screamed with pain. Her own claw came up, around Cheko's neck.

I lunged at them. All three of us splashed into the water.

I surfaced, whooshing air out of my lungs and water out of my gills. Grippers closed tightly on both my claw arms in a hold I could not break. Behind us, I could hear splashing and cursing, and I knew that the other Outsider was not having an easy time with Cheko.

The cresthead, clinging to me with both grippers, began to tow me back toward the skiff. I kicked and flailed. I couldn't let the Outsiders get Twig. But we moved closer and closer to the skiff, even though the current was pulling it steadily away.

"Help me here!" The other Outsider was holding Cheko under the water. "This one is worse than a wild sheemo."

My Outsider looked at the skiff. It was spinning a

little, with no one controlling it. She cursed. Then she turned and pulled me back. She released me with one gripper and grabbed Cheko's claw arm. Cheko screamed, but there was nothing she could do. With Cheko between the two of them, and me dangling behind, we swam back to the group waiting on the dock.

Eager grippers reached out and hauled me up. They dropped me, none too gently, onto the wet wood. Many reached to subdue Cheko, but when she was finally still, the Grown One made a gesture, and they released Cheko and let her stand upright. She wiped at all four arms with her grippers, as if she were wiping away something slimy and smelly. The Outsiders laughed, and one of them said, "By the Roots, she does have nerve."

"But what of the skiff, Mecha?" One of them pointed out into the river. I raised my head from the boards. The skiff was still floating downstream. Soon it would be carried around a small outreaching of land.

The Grown One closed her flaps. "The skiff is not our concern. We will not be accused of theft. We'll take them back to the Clearing and wait for Grandmother."

One of the wet crestheads grabbed me and hauled me toward the shore. No one touched Cheko, but several of them surrounded her and herded her along.

I glanced back as I stumbled off the end of the dock. The skiff had disappeared.

14
Mica

The Outsiders brought us to the center of their Clearing. There was a food house, a sleeping house, and a dining house, set farther back and away from the sheemo tank. But no dried tislit hung from the eaves, and the sand looked as if it had not been raked in seasons.

Cheko's tail twitched and brushed past my ankles. The crestheads were conferring in low voices. One of them left the group and grabbed my gripper arm. "You come with me."

"But . . ." I tried to resist, to drag my feet and fight, as I knew Cheko would do. But the cresthead was too strong for me.

She pulled me into the food house. A flathead was working inside. He looked up when we entered and promptly spilled shatalsha juice all over the floor. "You can't bring that in here!" he shouted, ignoring the puddle seeping into the sand.

"Mecha wants him confined. She said to bring him here." The cresthead sounded uncertain and defensive.

"Not in here." The flathead waved his claw, and the cresthead and I both took a step backward. "Don't you think I have enough to do, trying to keep all these mouths fed? I can't guard Outsiders, too."

"Mecha said—"

"Then I'll speak to Mecha." And he strode out the door.

"You're not taking this to Mecha without me!" The cresthead started to follow. Then she stopped. She stuck her head out the door and shouted, "Mica!"

A young cresthead, about my molting, appeared in the doorway.

"Stay here and watch this Outsider," the Grown One said.

The Young One's mouth opened as if to protest, but the Grown One had already hurried out the door.

I felt my tail begin to move, and I forced it to be still.

The Young One, Mica, stepped between me and the table. "Stay away from our food."

I let myself slide down the wall until I was sitting on the cool floor. I thought about Cheko, alone with so many. I thought about Twig, alone with no one. My head felt heavy, and I rested it against the wall.

"Are you all right?" Mica leaned closer to me. She reached out, and I flinched. She smiled and carefully dropped her gripper down at her side. "I'm not threatening you. Are you hurt?"

Before I could answer, two crestheads bustled in. One grabbed my claw arm and pulled me to my feet. "Come along. We have another place to keep you."

"I wouldn't touch your food anyway," I said over my shoulder as they hustled me out. "It smells." I couldn't tell whether Mica had heard me or not.

They had set up another tank next to the sheemos. The Outsiders grabbed my gripper arms and my legs and, with one smooth motion, tossed me inside.

I opened my gills and closed my mouth, but the tank was empty. I smacked against the rough bottom. A net was quickly stretched across the top.

I stood up, wincing a little at the new bruises. I jumped, grabbed the edge of the tank, and pulled myself up so I could see out into the Clearing. My head bulged the net, but the crestheads had fastened it securely. They were walking away, dusting their grippers and laughing. They disappeared into the dining house. I couldn't see Cheko anywhere.

Two small crestheads ran up. They stopped a few paces from the tank and stared at me. Then their grippers came out from behind their backs, and they pelted me with chlafa nodes. I sat down, out of sight.

I crouched near the wall, watching as more chlafas bounced into the tank, watching the shade chase the sun across the floor. There were almost enough chlafas to bake a decent-size loaf, and the shade had almost reached my toes, when I heard grippers fumbling at the net.

It was rolled back, and someone shouted, "Look out." I pressed back against the wall and just avoided having Cheko land on top of me.

She leapt up as soon as she hit the bottom. "You animals!" she shouted. "You're no better than animals!" But there was no answer.

"Are you all right? Did they hurt you?"

She looked at me, her claws still opened and her teeth bared, and for a moment she didn't even seem to recognize me. But then she relaxed and sat down.

"I'm fine," she said, and she sounded almost disappointed. "We sat in their dining house and stared at each other. They didn't even ask me any more questions. They just sat there, like dead tislit. And they smelled almost as bad, too."

"Probably waiting for their grandmother," I said, remembering the conversation on the dock.

Cheko hissed. "I don't even think they have a grandmother. I don't think they have any family at all. They're just a bunch of wild, uncivilized . . . Outsiders." She pointed a shaking digit at me. "Everything Uncle Simla ever said about them is absolutely true."

"Well, they haven't ripped us apart," I said.

"Not yet," she said. She looked around the tank. "What are all these chlafas doing in here?"

"They threw them at me. The Small Ones."

"Did they?" Cheko scooped up several of the largest nodes and hefted them in her gripper.

I soon heard the scuffling and the whispering. Cheko rose and moved toward the center of the tank, her flaps open. Then, suddenly, she unloosed her chlafas, sending them flying through the net. We heard a shriek and then cries of outrage.

"Ha!" Cheko said. She turned to me and grinned. "Got her!"

But the Small Ones were not easily defeated. By the time the sun was too low to enter the tank, we were almost ankle deep in chlafas.

Cheko cleared herself a space and sat down next to me. "I can't throw anymore. My gripper arm hurts."

"I'm not surprised."

"And I'm hungry."

I picked up one of the chlafas and took a small bite. I spat it out and wiped my tongue on my gripper.

"I'm certainly not hungry enough to eat raw chlafas," Cheko said. "And how can they expect us to sleep in a dry tank? Animals." She curled up and promptly fell asleep.

The sky darkened and the stars appeared. I could see the Claw and the Sheemo. I could hear Outsiders moving around the Clearing, doors opening and shutting. The cold had seeped into my blood, and I felt heavy and stupid.

"The one seed fell, in the rich and fertile soil of the one Clearing."

I held my breath. I might be back in our Clearing, with our stars, hearing Uncle Simla tell our story. But this did not sound like Uncle Simla, and I realized a cresthead was speaking.

"Are you hungry?"

I stood up, slow and stiff from the cold. I could see Mica through the net. She was sitting on the edge of the tank, peering down at me. "Let us go," I said. "Let us go home."

"Oh, hush." She glanced back over her shoulder. "The shutters are open. They'll hear you."

"I don't care if they hear me."

She held up two tislit from a pouch at her side. "I brought you something to eat. Even if it does smell." And her tongue flicked in a small, knowing smile.

I was hungry, painfully hungry, but I let the tislit fall without raising my grippers to catch them. One hit me on the head, but Mica didn't laugh. "Why did you come to our Territory?" she asked, and she sounded more curious than angry.

"We're traveling," I said. "My sister and I."

"I wouldn't mind having a brother," Mica said. She glanced behind her. "It would be better than all these sisters."

"I have another sister at home," I said. "A hatchling."

"A hatchling!" Mica turned back to me, and I was pleased to see her flared gills, pleased to see that I had surprised this Outsider, this cresthead. "A *new* hatchling?"

I blinked. "Healthy. And strong," I added. "She swam right into the tank."

"We haven't had a hatchling in seasons. Of course, we'd want a flathead . . ." Mica stopped, as if she'd said too much.

The silence stretched between us. I stared up at her claws, big claws for her age, with sharp points. I realized Mica had been looking at me looking at her claws.

"Well," I said, and my voice came out a little louder than I'd expected. "We were glad to get another cresthead. Another *strong* cresthead." I shuffled backward, and a chlafa popped under my talon, making a small, rude-sounding noise. I laughed—I couldn't help it—and Mica laughed too, her tongue unrolling. She didn't seem half so threatening when she laughed like that. My tail relaxed away from my feet and brushed one of the tislit. I picked it up, suddenly regretting my lack of manners, and took a small bite. It was spicy, but good. "How do the flatheads cook this?"

"*I* cooked it," Mica said, and she laughed again when my gills flared. "Grandmother says, in times of need, every gripper must work for the Family."

"That sounds like what my grandmother would say." I took another bite. "So how did you cook it?"

"Boiled. With chopped sheels."

I finished the tislit and licked my digits. "How many sheels?"

"Oh, about a gripper full. Chopped small."

"Shem!" Cheko jumped up and pushed between me and Mica. "Stay away, Outsider," she said, and her claws were open.

I picked up the other tislit and held it out to Cheko. "Try it. It's really good."

She shrank back, as if I were offering her sheemo dirt. But I could see her nostrils twitching at the good smell. She grabbed the tislit and ate it in big bites.

"Here." Mica dropped down two more.

I caught them and offered Cheko the biggest. She took it eagerly, and it was gone almost as quickly as the first. "Isn't it good?" I asked, around mouthfuls of my own.

She licked her digits. "Not too bad," she said.

"I can bring more," Mica said, looking at me, acting as if Cheko weren't there.

A door opened. "Mica!" The voice was loud and angry and close by. "Come down from there at once!"

Mica disappeared, as if she'd been pulled down. Then, suddenly, her head reappeared. "What's your name?" she whispered, pointing at me.

Cheko hissed, but I whispered, "Shem."

Mica blinked. "Shem," she said. She smiled and disappeared again.

Cheko had sat down against the wall. I sat beside her. Her gills were flared. "What was that all about?" she asked, finally.

"Nothing," I said. I ducked my head a little to look at my feet. "She shared her food," I said, as if I were mentioning the possibility of rain.

Cheko snorted like a sheemo. "She's still an Outsider, Shem. Don't forget that." She poked me, gently, with her claw. "But don't be afraid. I'm here to protect you." And she curled up and went back to sleep.

15
Terran Eyes

I hopped out as soon as the boat scraped against the bottom. I was lucky I'd drifted toward the shore and not out into the current. I looked around at the trees and the bushes. I hoped I was lucky, anyway.

I pulled the boat as far as I could out of the water, then I sat down in the wet sand, with my head on my knees. "Stay calm and analyze the situation."

My shoes and my pants were wet from wading ashore. I had bruises on my arms and my back from being stepped on. My lungs were burning again.

And I was all alone.

We'd been floating down the river. All the stuff I'd learned on the reality disc had come back to me, and I'd been doing well. It was pretty exciting in the fast part. The virtual boats hadn't had anything like that, but Little Claws had handled it great. I hadn't known why Big Claws had pushed me under the nets. But I hadn't been worried. Not until all the yelling started. And I didn't get really scared until the other Indigie climbed up and almost tipped the boat over.

That other Indigie hadn't seemed very friendly. I knew that it was wrong to judge things by our standards. The first lesson on the Cultural Arts comdisc was "Normal, inter-individual interactions among other life-forms may appear strange and even frightening to Terran eyes." I knew that by heart because I'd had to key it ten times on my compad. But how could I tell those were normal interactions? Little Claws and Big Claws had never yelled at each other, not like that. They'd never attacked each other.

The transponder was still beeping. I could hear it, could almost feel it, like a little heartbeat. I keyed the display. Visuals lit up the screen, coordinates, and directions, probably, and distances. I didn't know exactly how to read them, but I knew how the blinking arrow worked. "An idiot feature," Mom had said. "They're treating us like idiots again." I stood up and turned slowly in a circle. The arrow blinked when I faced upriver, the way we had come. It glowed steadily when I faced downriver. The other Terrans were somewhere downriver.

Walking would be easier than steering the boat. Maybe there was a path nearby.

I grabbed my pack and started through the bushes. They didn't grow as thickly here, and I did find a path right away. It was wide and well worn, a big path. It would take a lot of Indigies walking around a whole lot to make a path so wide and so deep.

I stepped out onto the broad open surface. I turned to my left and held the transponder out. The arrow was bright and steady.

I turned the other way, the way I figured was back up-river. The arrow started blinking like crazy. There was a funny sort of little hiccup every two or three seconds, and the screen would go completely blank.

I turned around and the numbers flashed and the arrow glowed. I turned back and the arrow blinked and then disappeared. "If the screen goes blank," Dr. Cynthia Wu had said, "this is a warning. You are heading in the wrong direction. You are heading away from the rest of your group."

I thought about the rest of my group. I knew they were really worried about me. Hanna who couldn't climb the ropes in gym. Hanna who couldn't access a comdisc even after she'd just finished studying it. I thought how great it would be to find Mom and Dad and Jeffrey. How great it would be to let someone else think up the plans and do the worrying.

And then I thought about Little Claws rubbing my head and making sure I was safely tied to the tree branches. I thought about him steering the boat around the big rock.

I stuck my silent transponder back in my pocket and started up the path, in the upriver direction. "This is the plan, Hanna," I said out loud. "Just find Little Claws and Big Claws. Make sure they're okay. All you have to do is make sure they're okay." And I was glad the other Terrans weren't there, because I wasn't sure this plan was a good one.

The sun slanted low through the branches, and it was almost cool here. The trees towered way up above me. It was very quiet. I felt like I was the only thing alive on this whole entire planet. I walked closer to the edge of the path. I tried to walk faster, but my lungs hurt too much, and I had to slow down.

I smelled the smoke first, so strong my nostrils stung. And another smell, familiar and fainter. Food sticks. It smelled like the food sticks cooking. I slowed my steps. The path stretched straight and then curved around a wide bend, about forty-five meters ahead of me. Maybe there was a city around that bend. Or a town, at least. They had to live somewhere, these Indigies.

I stopped completely. "Just think for a minute, Hanna," I said, and my voice sounded small and foreign. "Just try and think."

I looked around at the trees and bushes on either side of me. Just walking straight in along this path would be dumb. I couldn't speak their language. They couldn't speak mine. I was never totally on-line, not even when I was with Little Claws.

Maybe I could find a way to sort of analyze the situation before I was right in the middle of it.

I pushed my way off the path. The bushes scratched at my legs, and twigs caught in my clothes, but it wasn't too hard to get through. I tried to go quietly and carefully, following the smell of the smoke. Once I stopped, thinking I heard voices. But it was more like the creaky, branch-voice I'd heard up in the tree, and I decided my nerves were playing tricks on my ears.

In a few meters, I skirted one of those big trees. There was a box, like the one Little Claws and I had filled with fruit, but this one was empty and sort of beat-up. I rested beside it for a few minutes, getting my breath.

I pushed into the bushes, slowly creeping along, careful not to snap a twig or rustle through the leaves. I ducked under a taller bush and parted the branches. I had found where the Indigies lived. I sat down to analyze.

It wasn't anything like a city, or even a town. On Ravenna Prime, we wouldn't even have called it a commune. There were four or five huts set around a central, cleared, circular area. The huts had rounded roofs and walls. The walls looked like dried mud or clay. Each hut had one door, and two or three small windows. The smoke and the smells were coming from a small hut on my side of the clearing. Nearby were two big things that kind of looked like the fruit box, only they were taller and wider and not set on rollers. Something moved in the one nearest me, and water slopped over the side. The other box had a net tied over the top.

Indigies were moving around the clearing, going in

and out of the huts, talking to one another, carrying things. There were some littler ones, chasing one another around like they were playing some kind of game.

Watching them, I got a funny feeling in my stomach. Because—and I know I'm not supposed to even think this, I know that only Terrans who have never been off-world think stuff like this—but these guys all looked exactly alike. They all had claws and green and blue scales. They all had those big, staring eyes. When one of them went into a hut, I couldn't tell if the same one came out or a completely different one.

"Think, Hanna," I whispered. "And watch. Just keep an open mind."

Two of the little Indigies came sneaking around the side of one of the boxes. They were whispering. I could see their lips moving, but I couldn't hear them. All of a sudden, they threw something, rocks maybe, into the box. Then they ran off, hissing and squealing. And somebody inside the box shouted. And rocks came flying back out.

To Terran eyes, it looked pretty strange, all right. And I decided to wait until dark, to see for myself what was in that box.

Even though I was waiting for it, I was surprised when the sun went down, suddenly, the way it does. Lights came on in some of the windows, a funny, pale, flickering kind of light, not at all like lasers. The single moon was up, barely showing over the trees.

One of the Indigies came outside. He climbed up on the edge of the box with the netting over it. I could see him drop something down inside. Stick food, maybe? He sat there on the box for a while, until another Indigie came out and pulled him down.

I dug in my pack, and I ate some food and drank some water. I waited until everything was quiet and still, until everything had been quiet and still for a long time. I waited until the big moon and its satellite were up and lighting the clearing. I didn't want the Indigies to see me, but I really didn't want to go creeping around in the pitch dark, either.

The outside of the box was rough, and it was easy for me to pull myself up on the rim. Two Indigies were sitting inside. One of them looked up at me. "Shh," I whispered.

I could see big eyes and a big mouth. And then he made that sound he makes when he talks to me. "Hanna." And he stuck his big ugly tongue out. And I didn't know why I'd ever been afraid I wouldn't recognize him. I knew it was Little Claws for sure.

I put my finger on my lips, to tell him to be quiet, and then I started getting rid of the net.

Little Claws woke up Big Claws, and they stood up and watched me untie the knots and roll the net back. When I had an opening big enough for them to climb through, Little Claws reached up his hand and I grabbed it and helped him out. Then, together, we pulled Big Claws out.

We all dropped down onto the sand. I could have hugged them, would have hugged them both. But I knew we didn't have any time.

Big Claws said something, his voice sharp even in a whisper, and he pointed toward the bushes.

"I know the way," I whispered. "I'll go first." I started around the box. I looked back over my shoulder to make sure they were on-line and following me. And I ran smack into the claws of an Indigie coming the other way.

16
Rescue

Cheko butted Mica with her head. Tislit flew everywhere, and the two crestheads sprawled in the dirt. Then Cheko was on her feet. "Come on, come on, come on!" She pushed into the mehtas, and Twig and I pushed after her.

The mehtas were thick. We snapped branches and crunched leaves, and I knew we were making a lot of noise, too much noise. I opened my flaps, straining to hear the angry shouts, the sounds of pursuit. I thanked the Roots when we finally stepped free of the undergrowth, onto an open path.

"This way!" Cheko shouted. "Hurry!" And she started to run in the sunward direction. I grabbed Twig's gripper and ran after Cheko as fast as I could.

The Lasha Moon had long since climbed to the Roots. The Sheemo Moon and its hatchling were still high in the Great Shatalsha, though, pouring their cold, pale light along the path, like spilled sheemo oil. The cold wrapped around my body, thickening my blood, making me slower and stupider with each step. Twig pulled his gripper from mine and grabbed my claw arm, trying to tug me along faster. He looked up into my face, and he said something, his voice raspy and hurried. He held up his lasha box, and I could see the lights winking across its face. It didn't help. It was as cold as the moonlight. He put his arm around my waist, between my claw arms and my gripper arms. His body radiated a damp heat. I leaned against him and tried to soak up as much as I could.

Soon even Cheko had to slow down. And then she stopped in the middle of the path, her tail wrapped tight against her legs, whether from fear or for warmth, I couldn't tell. "Where are we?" She was scanning the path behind us, watching for Mica's aunts, I knew. Her claws opened and closed, opened and closed.

"You said we should go this way. I thought you knew where we were going." I faced the way we had come, too, my mind overgrown with images of angry crestheads rushing out of the darkness.

"I was just getting us away from the Clearing, sheemo brain." Cheko stopped watching the path and looked at me. "Don't tell me we're lost, Shem."

Lost? We couldn't be lost. Not in another Family's Territory. Not so far from our own Clearing. I tried to force my brain to think, to think clearly. "We need to find the river," I said. "If we can find the river . . ."

Twig had stepped away from me. He tugged at my claw arm and pointed into the underbrush. His other gripper held the lasha box up high. He pointed into the mehtas again. I looked behind us again. Could he hear the Outsiders coming? Maybe those fat, immobile ears could hear sounds our flaps missed.

Cheko hissed. "What now?"

"I think he wants us to hide . . ."

Twig hissed, almost exactly like Cheko, grabbed my claw arm and dragged me into the mehtas.

"Hey!" Cheko shouted. "Wait for me!" And I could hear her trampling along behind us.

We didn't have to go very far. Twig pulled me out of the mehtas onto a thin strip of sandy beach, running right along the river. And there, waiting for us, was the skiff.

Twig said something. But before Cheko and I could move, Mica stepped out of the mehtas. Her big claws were wide open. She didn't look slow and stupid. She looked angry. Very angry. Cheko moved in front of me, and her claws opened, too. "Stay out of the way, Shem," she said. And she waited for Mica to attack.

Mica stepped toward Cheko. Behind me, Twig hissed and said something. He was holding up the lasha box and all its lights for Mica to see, too. He was talking and talking, the words tumbling and bumping out like ripe shatalsha from a picking bag.

Mica stopped in her tracks. She stared at Twig with her gills flared and her mouth open.

Twig held the box up close to my face, and then, before I could stop him, he thrust it into my gripper.

The box was cold and hard, and I nearly dropped it, but I could feel the voice, pulsating inside it, like something alive.

Twig was still talking. He turned my body downriver, and I saw the light on the lasha box bloom and grow. And then he turned me upriver and the light faded and died. Downriver, blooming and growing. Upriver, fading and dying. And Twig's voice filling my flaps, his digits scratching my scales, the pale sides of his eyes shining in the moonlight.

I looked at Cheko and Mica. They were standing side by side, their claws closed and their mouths closed and their gills flared. "What are you doing?" Cheko asked, and her voice was soft and hesitant.

I opened and closed my flaps. "I . . . I don't know." I held out the lasha box. "Do you want to try it? It's kind of pretty." They both stepped back, Cheko treading on Mica's feet, and Mica not seeming to notice.

Twig grabbed the lasha box from me and fastened it back at his waist. Then he crossed to the skiff and pushed it into the water. He looked back over his shoulder and said something.

Cheko spun and shoved Mica, hard, into the mehtas. She shoved me toward the skiff. I fell in and Cheko tumbled in after me. Twig pushed us out into the current and jumped in, too.

I looked back at the shore to see if Mica was all right. But she was pulling herself up and into the skiff.

"Hey!" Cheko shouted, and she lashed out with her claw. "Get out!"

But Mica was too big for Cheko to dislodge, and she rolled into the bottom of the skiff. "I'm coming with you."

"No you're not!"

"Yes I am!"

Their claws were opened and grasping, their necks and faces coloring, their teeth bared. Twig stood, holding up his pole as if he were ready to hit someone.

"Wait, wait." I shifted over in between the two crest-heads. "It's all right," I said to Twig, and I made soothing motions with my gripper.

The skiff settled in the water. Cheko and Mica crouched on either side of me, their claws open but down.

"I'm not going to hurt you," Mica said, and Cheko hissed. "But I am coming with you."

"No you're not," Cheko said again.

"Try to stop me."

"I'll throw you out," Cheko said, and she lunged, and the skiff rocked and Twig yelped.

"Stop it!" I shouted as loud as I could. "Do you want to sink us? Sit down!" I was surprised when they both did sit, settling onto the nets like Small Ones reprimanded at the food table. I took a deep breath and turned to Mica. "Why do you want to come with us?"

Mica smiled. "You're the most interesting thing that's

happened in this forest since my uncle found a yala shaped like an elma."

"What a stupid reason!" Cheko said. She grabbed my claw arm, and her digits clenched so hard they hurt. "We can't take an Outsider with us."

"Well, we can't throw her out into the water."

"Why not?"

Because she shared her food. Because I don't want to throw her out, I thought. But I said, "Because she'll go back and tell her aunts where we are. We need to keep her here with us."

Cheko opened and closed her flaps, but she said, "Like a hostage, you mean?"

I blinked, although I didn't really know what I meant. "Exactly. Like a hostage."

Mica laughed out loud. "Did you know that you have a smart brother, Outsider?"

"Don't call my brother smart, Outsider."

"Cheko," I said.

Mica pointed at Twig, poling away behind Cheko. "Is he your brother, too?"

I had to use both my grippers to hold Cheko down. "He's not my brother," she spat out.

"Then what is he?"

"He's . . . he's . . ." Cheko looked at me, and we all looked at Twig, who showed us his teeth.

"We found him," I said, finally. "In the forest."

Mica didn't say anything for a moment. Then she

opened and shut her flaps. "Your Territory must be a lot more interesting than ours," she said.

"And you can just stay out of it, Outsider," Cheko said.

I put my gripper on her claw. "We're taking Twig to the Council Clearing," I said.

Mica blinked like this made sense. "My grandmother is at the Council," she said. "There was a call."

"They came to our Clearing, too, and . . . ouch!" I pulled Cheko's claw tip out of my arm.

"You don't have to tell her everything," Cheko said.

"I was just being polite."

"You aren't supposed to be polite to hostages."

She clicked and Mica clicked and I hissed. Trapped between two crazy crestheads. I thought about crawling into the bow to help with the poling, but my muscles were still stiff and cold. The river was wide and calm, and Twig had the skiff under control. His head bobbed up and down a little as he poled. The sun was beginning to climb behind him, and I welcomed its light and its warmth.

"Look!" Mica pointed out over the water, and we all looked, even Twig. "A tislit just jumped!"

"It *must* be boring in your Territory," Cheko said. "Tislit jump all the time."

"It did look like a big one," I said.

"Sometimes a tislit jumping is exciting, lasha lips," Mica said, leaning over me to look at Cheko. "Especially when the walk's been poor."

"Oh," I said. "We have lots of tislit this season," and I felt a bud of guilt, remembering the tislit we had eaten in the sheemo tank, and the ones Cheko had made Mica drop.

"My grandmother says that, a long time ago, the Families shared their extra food." Mica was looking across the water, and her voice reminded me of Uncle Simla's when he told a story. "She says the Families came together often, to trade and to talk. She says a person could live with whatever family she wanted, wherever she was needed." Mica paused and looked at Cheko and me, her eyes reflecting the climbing sun. "And Grandmother says all the eggs hatched."

Cheko laughed out loud. "Oh, pull my other tail, Outsider," she said. "Families sharing? Living anywhere? If it was so perfect, why would they have bothered to set up the Territories?"

"I didn't say it was perfect," Mica began, but, behind us, Twig shouted. He was holding his pole high, pointing ahead with his other gripper.

We all turned as one, and looked at the huge dock, stretching along the riverbank. And all the skiffs bobbing beside it.

"The Council Clearing," Cheko and Mica said together.

And we all sat and watched as Twig poled the boat right on past.

17
Enormous Claws

They looked up at me, and Big Claws shouted something. He pointed at the shore, back at the big long dock we'd just passed, and I could tell he wanted me to go back, to turn around. Although that was pretty silly. The current was way too fast for me to turn around. There was no way I could make this boat go anywhere but straight down the river.

Which was exactly where we were supposed to be going. "It's okay," I said, and I hoped I sounded reassuring. "We're going the right way."

Big Claws moved toward me, and the boat rocked and tipped. Little Claws yelled, and it was all I could do to keep us straight and upright. "You guys have to stop jumping around!" I shouted. "Just sit still!" And they did, for about two seconds.

Then they started talking, their voices going up and

down and getting louder. All three of them, even New Claws, talking at once. Big Claws gave Little Claws a shove, and he said something, then said something to me, and he pointed back behind us, too.

I sighed, and New Claws stuck out his feathery fans. I pointed ahead of us. "Terrans," I said, loudly and slowly. "*This* way." And they all turned, like mobicoms, as if there really was something to see besides water and trees.

I sighed again, and shoved the pole down, ducking to avoid the low-hanging branches. I didn't have time to bring them on-line, even if I could. The sun was coming up. I could feel its heat on the back of my legs. The light was changing from the yellow moonlight to the blue-white light the sun gave off. It made me nervous, to see how time was passing, now that I knew they were really here. Now that I knew I was so close. What if the Terrans decided to leave? What if they decided they'd waited long enough? What if we floated around this next big curve just in time to see a pod taking off, taking off without me?

We floated around the curve, and my heart jumped into my throat. An escape pod was pulled up on the beach, looming up over one of those docks, like some . . . well, like some alien spacecraft. But the lights were dark and the engines were off. I could tell no one was aboard.

Little Claws and Big Claws and New Claws were all staring at the pod with their fans open. Then they looked at me. "I told you so," I said. "I told you it wasn't back there."

They looked at the pod again, and then all three of them moved back, toward me. The nose of the boat came up out of the water. "Hey! Don't drown us now!"

I poled the boat over and bumped it against the dock. I was sort of proud of how I'd managed to keep from bashing it against the wood. But no one congratulated me. They were still staring at the pod. "I have to go find my family," I said. And that made them all start arguing again. I climbed over them and jumped out onto the dock.

I didn't bother to tie the boat up, or to wait for the Indigies, or anything. I ran along the dock and across the beach to the path that led into the forest. I could hear the Indigies running after me. I had the transponder in my hand, and it was easy to follow the signal. I was going to see Mom and Dad. And Jeffrey. And Andrea Hadaka. Good old Andrea Hadaka. Right at the fork and right again, and there was a clearing in the trees.

I stopped so fast that Little Claws and Big Claws ran right into me and nearly knocked me flying. It was a clearing, all right. With little round huts, and the same smell of smoke and cooking. But there weren't any Terrans.

The clearing was pretty well filled up with Indigies. They had been sitting in little clumps, arranged in sort of a rough circle. But when they saw us, and they all seemed to see us at about the same time, they stood up. All their fan-things came out at once, like a comdisc I saw once of a bunch of Terran Indigies. Birds, I told myself. "They were called birds." But these Indigies didn't rise up into the air. They all just stood there, looking at us.

Big Claws and Little Claws and New Claws were all behind me. I glanced back and saw they weren't going anywhere, either. They were kind of huddling behind me, like I was supposed to hide them.

I could feel the panic starting to rise inside me. I'd brought us to completely the wrong place. I'd brought us someplace that wasn't safe for any of us. Not for me, and not for them. Stupid, stupid Hanna.

One of the Indigies was moving out of the circle, moving toward us. He was tall and had really big claws. Hanna meets Enormous Claws, I thought, and hysterical laughter bubbled up inside of me. Enormous Claws said something, and his voice was deep and loud, and the laughter died before it could get out of my mouth. I took a step back, but the Indigies behind me were pushing me forward. Enormous Claws said something else, something that sounded sort of familiar. And Little Claws and Big Claws stepped out from behind me, and they answered him.

Another big Indigie had stepped out and was talking, and now New Claws was out in front and he was answering.

And then I realized that the big Indigie was pointing

at me, pointing and talking. They all looked at me. Little Claws and Big Claws and New Claws and all the other claws. Only twenty of them, maybe, I saw now. Not so many. But all of them looking at me. Waiting for me to say something, waiting for me to answer.

Only I didn't know what to say. I couldn't just start babbling away about Mom and Dad. But they all kept looking and waiting. So, finally, I pointed at Little Claws. I had to clear my throat a couple of times, because it was dry, and I wished I hadn't left my water in the boat. But I finally managed to say the one word I could say in their language. I said, "Little Claws."

It was as if a huge wind came along and blew them all back one step. And their fans got even bigger. And I thought, Oh, good job, Hanna. You said it wrong. Or you said something bad. And I could feel myself blushing, the heat moving across my cheeks. And some of their neck fans colored and darkened, and they were moving toward me with their claws open.

But Little Claws stepped beside me. His tongue flicked out. Smiling, I thought. Not breathing fast. Smiling and trying to make me feel better. He pointed to me, and he said, "Hanna," or the word that means Hanna, and I wondered just exactly what he did call me. No Claws? Maybe I was No Claws. And I was so relieved, I put my hand on his arm and I laughed out loud.

Something big banged on the door of the little hut closest to us. "Hanna!" someone shouted, and it was my real name, not shushes and sighs and hisses. "Hanna! Is that you?"

"Dr. Wu?" I shouted.

A big Indigie said something, and two of them lifted a bar off the door of the hut. The door opened, and Dr. Cynthia Wu, in full spacesuit and helmet, stepped out into the sunlight.

Never in a million years would I have done this back on the *Turing,* but now I ran over to Dr. Wu, and I threw my arms around her, and I hugged her.

It was sort of a clumsy hug, because of her suit. I stepped back and tried to see around her, into the hut. "Mom? Dad?"

"They're not here with me, Hanna," Dr. Wu said. She was looking over my head, watching the Indigies. "A mission of this kind requires only one search vessel equipped with a good com—"

I reached up and grabbed the sides of the seal ring and pulled her head down, forcing her to look at me. "Where are my parents?" I said loudly and slowly, like I was talking to Little Claws. "Where is my little brother?"

She blinked, and her eyes looked watery and distorted behind the faceplate. "They're back on the *Turing,* of course. They're waiting for me to bring you back."

For a second, I thought maybe Dr. Wu had completely erased her files. "But the *Turing* blew up or something. The pods were all ejected."

Now finally she really did look at me. "Oh, no,

Hanna. That was just a com malfunction. Your pod was ejected by mistake. Everyone else is still back on the ship. Safe and sound."

"By mistake!" I let go of her suit and stepped back. "A com malfunction!" I was shouting, and the Indigies closest to us muttered and clicked, but I didn't care. "I've been stuck here all alone because of some com malfunction?"

"Now, Hanna." Dr. Wu's voice was loud, but she took a deep breath, and I knew she was telling herself to keep calm. She put her heavy, gloved hands on my shoulders and looked down at me, but her eyes kept flicking up to the Indigies. "You did surprisingly well by yourself. Better than test scores would have predicted."

I took a deep breath, too. It wasn't her fault, I thought. It wasn't anybody's fault. "Yeah," I said. "I did all right."

Dr. Wu smiled. "The important thing is that you're safe, and I've found you."

"I found you," I said, and I wiggled her hands off my shoulders.

She frowned. "The incidence of large flora was much greater than I anticipated." She waved her hand at the forest. "The trees. Statistically, you wouldn't have expected so many trees."

I nodded. "There are a lot of trees."

"And then, these . . . these . . ." She fluttered her other hand at the Indigies.

I turned and looked at them, too. The ones closest to us were watching us, and I didn't like the way their claws kept opening and shutting. But the rest had formed back into their circle, and it sounded like they were arguing. They seemed to argue a lot, these Indigies.

"Once I had landed, I came to their . . . village, following the proper protocols. To explain my intentions and my mission." Dr. Wu paused. "They locked me up." She sounded like Jeffrey when Mom grounded him for something I'd done.

"They left me in a tree," I said. "But I think it was a mistake."

"Do you know the probability of finding an indigenous, sentient life-form?" Dr. Wu was shaking her head.

"Infinitesimal," I said. "But they are. Sentient, and everything else." I could see Little Claws now, standing on the other side of the circle.

"Well, we can certainly write this planet off for future colonization," Dr. Wu said. "Poor oxygen-to-nitrogen ratios. Crazy Indigies."

I felt a sudden wave of anger. I frowned up at her. "They're not crazy. They're really okay, once you get used to them." And I knew that, as much as I wanted to get off this planet, I was going to miss these guys. I was going to miss Little Claws.

Dr. Wu's face distorted into her teaching face. "Hanna. Locking up other sentient beings is not 'okay.'"

I pointed at the comtrans on her wrist. "What about

that? Why don't you just use that to tell them we want to go back to the pod? Tell them we want to go home."

She tapped the comtrans with her finger. She looked funny, and it took me a second to figure out she was embarrassed. "I don't think it's working," she said. "It was really designed for Terran-based languages. I'll have to try some recalibrations when we get back to the *Turing.*"

I put my hands on my hips. "We can't just stand here and wait for the Indigies to figure out what we want!"

I knew I was getting loud again, because the Indigie by the hut wall poked his claw out at me. I made a face at him, and he hissed and stepped back.

Dr. Wu put her glove on my arm. She tried to smile at the Indigie, but it didn't come out too well. "Hanna. Access the first rule. Stay—"

"Calm," I said. I shook my head. "Dr. Wu. Sometimes you have to do more than stay calm."

I grabbed her hand, and I pulled her out of the doorway. I pulled her through the crowd of Indigies, across the circle, all the way over to Little Claws.

18
Star Climbing

Twig stood in the doorway of the sleeping house, talking to the other hatchling. This one still wore the pale, puffy outer covering, but I could tell he was bigger than Twig. A Grown One, I thought, and I turned to Cheko to tell her, to say, see he *does* have a Family.

But Mother had pulled Cheko to one side. "Why are you here?" I had never seen Mother so angry, and I was glad she had hold of Cheko and not of me.

"The shatalsha told me to come," Cheko said, her grippers and her claws tight-closed at her sides. "The shatalsha told me to bring him to the Council Clearing."

That silenced them all. Not just Mother and Grandmother and Aunt Kichel, but the Outsiders closest to us as well.

"You heard the shatalsha, Cheko?" Grandmother said at last.

Cheko blinked.

"Why would they concern themselves with these clawless creatures?" Mother asked.

"It does no good to question the shatalsha." Grandmother was still staring at Cheko. "Then why didn't you stop at the Council Clearing?"

Cheko's tail twitched, but her voice was firm. "That was Shem's fault. *He* wasn't poling the skiff." My fault! And she had promised! I unloosened my tongue to protest, but Cheko knew when she had the advantage. She pointed at Mother. "Why aren't *you* at the Council Clearing?"

Mother hissed. "The Council was interrupted by these Outsiders, this family, demanding that we come to their Clearing to see the Outsider from the Sky."

"I thought . . ." My voice died when I saw them all looking at me, but I forced myself to go on. "I thought you were going to the Council because of Twig, because of the Outsiders from the Sky." They were all looking at me, staring at me like an elma that's suddenly begun to speak. I turned to Cheko. "*You* said they were talking about Twig."

"We came to the Council," Grandmother said, "to discuss the loss of our eggs and the death of the hatchlings."

"Flatheads need not hear talk of this," Mother said, and she stepped forward, as if to hide us from the eyes of the Outsiders.

Grandmother raised her gripper. "It is time we all

heard talk of this," she said, and her voice was loud enough for all the flaps nearby to catch her words.

Aunt Kichel hissed. "And we should have stayed and discussed the eggs, instead of running through the cold forest in the middle of the night to stand here and argue and do nothing."

I thought of all the Old Ones and the crestheads, running through the forest in the dark, their council cloaks flapping, and I almost smiled.

"We can't have Outsiders in our forest," one of the other Old Ones said, as if she were a part of our conversation.

"Strange Outsiders, you mean," said a cresthead.

"Unnatural Outsiders," another said.

Mother hissed. "We can't start this again."

"I say drown them and be done with it," said the cresthead, and I saw eyes blinking in agreement and relief.

Drown them? "Cheko," I whispered, "we can't just . . ." Something tugged at my arm. I looked down into tislit eyes, looking up into mine. "Twig!"

Grandmother and Mother and Aunt Kichel all stepped back, away from Twig and his Grown One, who stood close behind him. Twig said something, and all the crestheads stepped back farther, bumping into one another in their haste to give us room, to make a large circle around us.

Twig spoke, and his soft digits grabbed tight onto my

claw arm. He knelt, pulling me down with him, and began clearing a place in the dirt with his other gripper. I could feel the crestheads shuffling closer around us, jostling to see. I could feel their fear, moving closer with them. But I wasn't afraid. Not of Twig. His Grown One said something, and he answered without looking, his eyes on me. He said my name, and I smiled, and he began to draw.

"This is no time for games," Aunt Kichel said, but Grandmother shushed her.

Twig finished his drawing. He sat back and looked at it. And then he looked at me.

If we had been playing Next Line, I could have guessed after the first line, and I would have won right away. It was a picture of the star, the star on the riverbank. But I knew we weren't playing Next Line.

"You want to go to that star," I said. I pointed over his head, toward the path, and the Outsiders shuffled aside, as if my digit had the force to move them.

Twig's head bobbed.

I stood up. Twig stood, too, and his gripper slid into mine. I turned until I found Grandmother, standing behind Cheko. "They want to go to their star," I said, and, when I saw they didn't understand, I added, "to the thing back on the riverbank."

"That's not a star," someone said, before Grandmother could answer. "Stars are smaller."

"And brighter," someone else said.

I thought about the inside of the star. "It might be a

kind of skiff," I said, and I closed my flaps, expecting their laughter, but they were all silent.

Twig's gripper moved in mine, but he didn't pull it free. He reached out with his other gripper, grasped the sleeve of the Grown One's covering, and pulled him closer. The Grown One bent down and said something, and Twig looked up into the round, blank face. And I knew something. Something I should have known from the very beginning. "I think they want to leave," I said. "They want to go back to their Family."

Again I thought the crestheads would laugh, but the silence was so complete I could hear the twitching of their tails.

Grandmother stepped forward. She looked at the faces around her. "We must stop thinking with our claws. The Family from the Sheemo Rock says we must take the Outsiders from the Sky to their star."

Mica's grandmother blinked. "The Family from the Rapids agrees."

Another Old One, the one with the mottled crest who had been in our Clearing said, "If it means they will be gone from our forest, the Family from the Three River Curves agrees as well."

"Come on," I said to Twig. "Quick. Before they start arguing again." I tugged at his gripper, and he and his Grown One followed me. Across the Clearing and down the path. And I knew all the others were following as well.

When we reached the beach, Twig's Grown One

moved ahead of me. He looked bigger out in the open, taller and more threatening. He said something, and his voice was deep and hollow, like a sheemo's. He moved off toward the star.

Twig pulled his gripper from mine and started after. Then he stopped and turned. He said, "Shem," and he came and put his thin arms around me, the way he had done up in the shatalsha, the way he and his Grown One had done at the sleeping house door. And I put all my arms around him, careful to keep my claws closed and the hooks pointed out, so I wouldn't scratch him. I glanced back at the crestheads. "You'd better go," I said.

The Grown One had opened the star's door. He shouted something and climbed inside. Twig pulled away from me. Then he placed his gripper flat on my chest. He said something.

"I'll miss you, too, Twig," I said, and I touched the moss on his head, and I smiled.

Then slowly and carefully, he stuck his stubby little tongue out in a big smile.

I laughed out loud, and he showed me all his teeth. Then he turned and ran to the star. He paused at the door and waved his gripper over his head. Then he disappeared inside, the door swooshing shut after him.

Immediately the star began to rumble and roar, shaking with its own noise. I heard shouts behind me, but I didn't move. I watched the star slide down the beach into the river, making the water boil and foam. It turned beyond the end of the dock, and then, suddenly, it was skimming above the water, moving down the river, rising farther and farther into the air. It rose above the talfas and above the shatalshas, dwindling rapidly, until it was barely the size of a mechaka. And then no more than a point of light, climbing back up the Great Shatalsha.

I felt Cheko's gripper on my arm. "Well, he *was* more interesting than a big tislit," she said.

I turned and looked at all the crestheads standing on the beach, families all mixed together, Outsiders with Outsiders. I had never seen crestheads so silent before. And then, they stirred and shifted and moved back into their Family groups, each group separated from the others by a small strip of bare sand.

An Old One stepped forward. "It is time we returned to the Council Clearing."

And, like tislit suddenly freed from a broken net, all the Outsiders moved toward the path, as if Twig and his Grown One had already been forgotten. But what can you expect from crestheads, I thought.

"We can't leave the skiff here," Aunt Kichel said. She was staring at the dock, her grippers on her claws. "How will we get it back upriver?"

"We would offer our help." Mica and her grandmother and two other crestheads had not left the riverbank. They were standing in a small cluster. Mica's grandmother extended her flattened gripper. "After the Council, my daughters will pole your skiff back to our dock. We will keep it there until members of your Family can come to move it back into your territory."

"Be sure to send Shem back," Mica said. One of the crestheads hissed, but Mica smiled at me. And, even though they were all watching, I smiled back.

They crossed the beach toward the path. Mica looked back once, and I heard Cheko click her claw.

"It would seem, Shem-la, that you have made a friend." Grandmother was looking at me.

"A friend?" Mother's tongue slipped on the unfamiliar word. "What does *friend* mean?"

Grandmother still stared at me. "Friend is an ancient word. An ancient word too long unused." She looked at Mother. "It means an Outsider who is like Family."

Friend. I turned the word over in my mind, enjoying its shape and its feel.

"We must go also," Grandmother said. "There is much for the Council to discuss."

She and Mother and Aunt Kichel began walking toward the path. Cheko hit me with the flat of her claw. "I saw the way you were looking at that Mica's claws."

"You have to admit, she is good-looking."

"For an Outsider."

"For anybody."

Cheko hissed. "You have chlafas for brains, Shem." She started up the beach, then stopped and pointed at me. "I hope you don't think you're going back there alone. I'm going to be keeping my eye on you and that

Mica," she said, and she ran to catch up with Grandmother.

I stood for a moment, staring at the place where Twig's star had rested. Then I walked over to the dock and down its length to our skiff. His pouch was still there, under the nets. I dumped the food out into the water, watching it sink to the bottom. The tislit would like it. Tislit ate anything. I slid the pouch strap over my shoulder. It was small, but it would be good for carrying mehta berries. And memories.

Then I hurried to catch up with my Family.